Readers love

"A book as warm and radiant ..."
Lisa Thompson, author of *The Goldfish Boy*

"An utterly brilliant book that had me laughing and
crying in equal measure."
Tolá Okogwu, author of *Onyeka and the Academy
of the Sun*

"A beautiful, heartwarming hug of a book about the
power of self-acceptance. I defy anyone not to fall in love
with Sunshine!"
Hannah Gold, author of *The Last Bear*

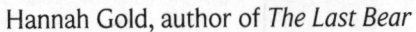

"A delightful story that manages to be both sincerely heartfelt and
sparklingly funny in equal measure."
L.D. Lapinski, author of *The Strangeworlds
Travel Agency*

"This uplifting and charming middle-grade is warm and funny.
It puts a spotlight on the Windrush generation and has the most
wonderful grandpa! You'll love it."
A.M. Dassu, author of *Boy Everywhere*

"A huge, uplifting hug with a message that says:
be yourself; be proud of who you are."
Jen Carney, author of *The Accidental Diary of B.U.G.*

"Sunshine lives up to her name – she's charming
and hilarious."
Aisha Bushby, author of *A Pocketful of Stars*

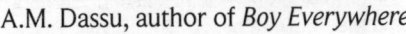

"This is a very special book."
Serena Patel, author of *Anisha, Accidental Detective*

"Powerful and poignant, hilarious and heartwarming.
I'm just so in love with this book."
Rashmi Sirdeshpande, author of *How To
Be Extraordinary*

For my Aunt Grace, the Peart family, and all of my Jamaican relatives

First published in the UK in 2024 by Usborne Publishing Limited, Usborne House, 83-85 Saffron Hill, London EC1N 8RT, England, usborne.com

Usborne Verlag, Usborne Publishing Limited, Prüfeninger Str. 20, 93049 Regensburg, Deutschland VK Nr. 17560

Text copyright © G. M. Linton, 2024.

The right of G. M. Linton to be identified as the author of this work has been asserted by her in accordance with the Copyright, Designs and Patents Act, 1988.

Cover and internal character illustrations by Fuuji Takashi © Usborne Publishing Limited, 2024.

Additional interior illustrations by Asma Enayeh © Usborne Publishing Limited, 2024.

The name Usborne and the Balloon logo are Trade Marks of Usborne Publishing Limited.

A CIP catalogue record for this book is available from the British Library.

ISBN: 9781801313360 7605/1 JFMAM JASOND/24

Printed and bound using 100% renewable energy at CPI Group (UK) Ltd, Croydon, CR0 4YY.

MIX
Paper | Supporting responsible forestry
FSC® C171272
www.fsc.org

SUNSHINE SIMPSON

Friends Always & Forever

G.M. LINTON

Illustrated by Fuuji Takashi and Asma Enayeh

USBORNE

Auntie Sharon

Dariuszkz
(aka Daz)

Ziggy

Great-Aunt Vi

Granny
Cynthie &
Grampie
Clive

Mum & Dad

Great-Aunt Jou

Meet my family — and welcome to my rollercoaster life!

Me

Grandad Bobby

Grandma Pepper

The Twinzies (Lena & Peter)

I have a large map of the world on my bedroom wall.

When I meet someone new, from a country other than the UK, I put a yellow dot on my map to mark the place they're from. It could be a big country like India or a smaller country, maybe somewhere like Barbados, where the singer Rihanna is from. (I like little bonus extra facts like that.)

Today was going to be different. This time, I'd be putting an extra special red dot on my map, because I was getting ready for an adventure of my very own.

I took my red dot and fixed my eyes on the Caribbean Sea, finding the island I was looking for. I carefully placed the red dot on the map, which swallowed the island whole.

The island may have looked small on the map, but from all I knew and had heard about it, it was far larger and brighter than any map could ever show.

My body tingled inside and out, through a mixture of nerves and excitement.

I chewed on my bottom lip, thinking about what my Grandad Bobby would tell me if he was here with me now. *"Go and have your own adventures."* That's exactly what he would have told me.

It was time...

Time for this girl to go **INTERNATIONAL**.

LUCKY NUMBER SEVEN (AND ELEVEN)

7, 14, 21, 28, 35 – 11.

These are the numbers that changed my family's life.

Last Christmas, in memory of her dad (my Grandad Bobby) my Auntie Sharon had played the Christmas lottery with the numbers that Grandad had always played with – and she won, **BIG TIME**.

Auntie Sharon had won **FOUR AND A HALF MILLION POUNDS**.

I'd always thought that when choosing lottery numbers, people picked special occasions like anniversaries and birthdays. But not my grandad. He believed that seven and combinations of seven were his lucky numbers. Though I wasn't sure where the number eleven had come from.

It turns out that Grandad was right about lucky number seven. And even though he was, sadly, no longer here to share the win, Auntie Sharon wanted to make sure that the rest of the family didn't miss out on enjoying her lottery-winning good fortune.

Once my family had finished an evening of non-stop screaming after we'd found out about the win, Auntie Sharon went on a "bit" of a spending spree.

She bought a MASSIVE four-bedroom house in a posh area of town called Poseley. Almost every room, including the four bathrooms, are decorated with animal-print velvet wallpaper and animal-print furniture to match. If you close your eyes and touch the wallpaper in Auntie Sharon's new house it feels like you're on safari. And when she wears animal print clothes to match her rooms, it's as if she's hiding in camouflage.

She also bought:

☀ A "racing red" sports car.

☀ A HUMUNGOUS diamond ring, which she'd flash

around while singing and doing the dance moves to Beyoncé's song "Single Ladies! (Put A Ring On It)" (even though she now has a nice boyfriend, called Dennis).

✳ Luxury food hampers from a famous, expensive shop in London called Harrods, which she had delivered to all her old neighbours and friends as if she was Mother Christmas.

✳ A speedboat.

"A SPEEDBOAT?" cried Mum when Auntie Sharon had shown us a picture of it in the brochure. "We live in the West Midlands. It's LANDLOCKED."

"What can I say? I feel the need for speed — and the boat is just so SHINY." Auntie Sharon's eyes shone brighter than her boat. "And PAH! Landlocked SCHMANDLOCKED! We have more miles of canals than Venice. There's plenty of room for me and my little speedboat."

Mum opened and closed her mouth like a goldfish but said nothing else.

That's the thing about my Auntie Sharon, she often leaves people speechless.

And another thing about my auntie is she's a very generous person. As well as also sharing her good fortune with local charities, and buying lots of other gifts for her family and friends, the **BEST** thing of all was her treating us — her son, Daz; my parents; my seven-year-old siblings, Peter and Lena (or The Twinzies as I like to call them because they are twins); Dad's parents, my Granny Cynthie and Grampie Clive; her boyfriend Dennis; and me — to a **HOLIDAY OF A LIFETIME**.

We'd be going to Jamaica for **THREE WHOLE WEEKS** during the summer holidays and staying in an all-inclusive five-star resort as part of the trip.

This was brilliant news, because not only would it distract me from thinking too much about high school, which I'd be starting in September and was beginning to get nervous about for reasons I'll get to, but visiting Jamaica was also the holiday of my dreams. We'd only ever been on holidays in Britain before — and never as a whole family.

These were epic times. Sun, sea — and **NO SCHOOL**!

I was so excited I thought my head might explode.

HOLIDAY MOOD

So now here we were, already two-and-a-bit weeks into the summer holiday and just a few days before we'd be jetting off to Jamaica. It was Friday evening, and we were leaving on the Monday morning.

As well as staring dreamily at Jamaica on my wall map of the world, I'd also been spinning my desk globe around so much, in giddy delight, that it had almost flown off its podium.

Mum kept popping her head into my bedroom, making tutting sounds and telling me I needed to finish packing my suitcase by the next day for checking, but I was just *so* busy with other **VERY IMPORTANT** stuff…

"Are you sure you don't want me to help you?" asked Mum, after her twentieth head-pop into my room. "I've added your toiletry bag, underwear and sandals into your case, but as you've INSISTED on packing the rest of your clothes yourself, I DON'T want us to enter into a last-minute scramble situation. AM I MAKING MYSELF CLEAR?"

Mum was both LOUD and clear.

I battled an outward sigh. "Mum, you worry too much. I'll be starting high school after the summer holidays. I'm practically a teenager, so I think I can manage to add my own clothes to a little old suitcase."

Mum's eyebrows sailed up towards the ceiling. "Hmm... We'll see," she said, in that doubting-Mum way of hers and walked off.

Oof, sometimes grown-ups have no faith.

I went back to not doing my packing. Instead, I decided to write some of the things that I'd researched — and that my grandparents had told me — about Jamaica into my Things and Places of Interest notebook, where I write about all the new people I meet from different parts of the world and exciting facts about new places I've never been to before. I just couldn't stop thinking about it, so writing things down helped me to feel like I was already there.

MY LIST OF EXCITING THINGS ABOUT JAMAICA:

✳ Jamaica is known as "the land of wood and water". It has gorgeous sunny weather, lush, green mountains and clear seas, and is known for some of the most beautiful beaches in the world. Sun, sea and sand (and green). Woo-hoo!

✳ Usain Bolt, who is a super-fast world record holder, is from Jamaica and Elaine Thompson-Herah and Shelley-Ann Fraser-Pryce are two of the fastest women sprinters ever. It's a speedy island!

✳ Jamaica is famous for reggae music and one of its most famous musicians is Bob Marley. Other famous musicians that my grandparents love are Jimmy Cliff, John Holt, Desmond Dekker, and Dennis Brown. Music is in Jamaica's heart and soul.

❋ Jamaican food is very tasty. Its national dish is ackee and saltfish, and then there's my favourite dish, brown stew chicken and fried dumplings. There's other great food too like jerk chicken, rice and peas, and curry patties as well as so much more. **YUM!**

❋ James Bond, 007, is Jamaican. Kind of. The writer of the James Bond books, Ian Fleming, wrote them in Jamaica, from his home called Goldeneye. (I'd be Sunshine Simpson 011 — because that's my age.)

❋ Even though it's a really hot country where it doesn't snow, Jamaica had a bobsled team go to the Winter Olympic Games in 1988. A film called *Cool Runnings* is inspired by the team's story. (Note to self: no need to bring ski boots on holiday to Jamaica.)

❋ Jamaica is around 22 times smaller than the United Kingdom. There are almost 68 million people living in the UK compared with nearly three million people who live in Jamaica. Jamaica is "likkle but tallawah", small but **STRONG**.

Just when I was getting into my flow, Mum called me downstairs.

I was expecting another nagathon about packing. If only I had a magic finger where I could just whisk things out of my drawers and into my suitcase. That would be much more fun – and so much quicker.

When I came down to the living room, Dad and Mum – who was finally taking a break from over-organizing our lives – were sitting next to each other on the sofa looking at photo albums.

"Hey, Sunny, we're just getting into the holiday mood by looking at these old pictures of family in Jamaica," said Dad.

"Yes, we thought you'd like to see them as you're taking your holiday research very seriously." Mum smiled. I grinned back at her. How did she know what we were up to almost all the time?

Flicking through one of the albums was like watching a film of Mum's and Auntie Sharon's lives when they were kids.

There were loads of pictures of them when they had

been a little younger than me, on holiday in Jamaica, smiling and wearing T-shirts and shorts while stuffing their faces at a beach barbecue, with corn on the cob as yellow as the sandy beach they were standing on. Then there were the photos, a few years on, where Mum looked like a sulky teenager, standing, with slumping shoulders, in between Grandad Bobby and my very glamorous grandmother, Glammy Pepper, as we call her.

Mum and Auntie Sharon went to live in Jamaica with my grandparents when they were teenagers, but they couldn't fully settle into life there, so Glammy and Grandad Bobby brought them home again. Mum doesn't really like to talk about that time, and she hasn't been back to Jamaica since.

"This is a picture of your Great-Aunt Joy, your grandmother's sister, on the veranda of her house. We'll be travelling to visit her and the rest of the family in Clarendon," said Mum.

I nodded. I knew all about the plan. Mum is very much one for planning things out to the smallest detail. I mean, what's wrong with freestyling sometimes? Mum needed to chill a bit more.

In the first week of the holiday, we'd be at the hotel. For the second week, we'd be visiting Glammy Pepper, Great-Aunt Joy and some of the rest of my Jamaican family on Mum's side for five days. Then for the third and final week of our holiday we'd be returning to the hotel, where Dad's side of the family in Jamaica would be joining us.

I was looking forward to staying at the hotel, but I was even more eager to get a slice of Jamaican life at my Great-Aunt Joy's place in Clarendon. Two of my Grandad Bobby's favourite singers, Freddie McGregor, who sings reggae songs, and Liz Mitchell, from a band called Boney M, who sang the famous Christmas song "Mary's Boy Child", were from Clarendon. And a man called Levi Roots, who's famous for being on Dragons' Den and making reggae sauces that you can buy in supermarkets is from there too. All part of my research! Would I see anyone famous on this holiday, like when my friend Evie saw the famous film star George Dooley when she went on holiday to Italy a few years ago? I giggled at the prospect of what lay ahead, even though I doubted I'd meet any superstars. I couldn't wait to meet some of my Jamaican relatives for the first time.

Mum then showed me photos of our cousin Lorna, Great-Aunt Joy's daughter, who Mum used to hang out with when she was in Jamaica. One photo showed Lorna when she was older, with a toddler balancing on her knee. The little boy was dressed in shorts, a smart shirt and a cap, which sat lopsided on his head, as if he'd tried to yank it off but failed. He was smiling broadly, through a glistening, dribbling mouth, and looked like he was mischievously trying to wriggle out of Lorna's firm grip.

"Who's that?" I asked.

"It's your cousin, Ziggy, of course. Lorna's son." Dad smiled. "Ziggy's thirteen now, so two years older than you. Hopefully you'll get to hang out with him. It'll be good for you to have company close to your own age."

The thought of meeting my older cousin for real, and not just saying a quick awkward hello on a phone call, which is what I had been used to doing at Christmas and Easter for as long as I could remember, was exciting but also a little nerve-racking too. Would we get on?

"And here's a photo up at Old Farm, your grandad's childhood home," said Mum, as she ran her finger gently across the photograph.

It was a colourful photo — dimmed slightly by age, but bright colours of orange, green and more still did their best to burst through. Mum, Auntie Sharon, Glammy Pepper and Grandad Bobby stood next to a tall mango tree. Its branches were bursting with the tender fruit. There was a small woman, wearing a cap and a T-shirt that had the words "Jamaica — No Problem" written on it, standing next to them.

"Is that Grandad's sister?" I asked.

"Yes, that is your Great-Aunt Vi." Mum smiled. "She still lives up at Old Farm with her family. We'll go and visit them too, while we're in Clarendon... So much to do and still so much to organize." Mum sighed, her mind wandering back to suitcase packing, no doubt.

I'd never met any of my Jamaican family in person. But my mind was opening to seeing these distant people for real. Would Ziggy have the same big smile he did as a baby — but hopefully not the dribbly mouth? It was like having a whole different part of yourself — your history — somewhere else in the world and I was here for it.

"Have Lorna or Great-Aunt Joy ever visited England?" I asked.

"Lorna came over for our wedding," said Mum with a smile. "She saved really hard and other family members, including Aunt Joy, and my mum and dad, helped out with her plane fare. I was so grateful that she could make it."

"Didn't you want to go back to Jamaica for your honeymoon?" I was peppering Mum and Dad with questions. I must have asked that one a bit abruptly because Mum seemed startled by it.

"Well," said Dad, taking over the conversation. "As Lorna had come all the way to England for the wedding, we spent some time showing her around. And then, after Lorna returned to Jamaica, we had a long weekend in sunny Spain. It was lovely."

"Even though it rained every day — so it ended up more like soggy Spain," said Mum, with a rueful smile.

"But we still had each other, so that was all right," said Dad, a bit too soppily for my liking. "We just never got round to going back over to the land of wood and water.

What with life, work…just big people boring stuff. Until now, that is. But, no regrets." Dad reached over and gently squeezed one of Mum's hands.

"No regrets," said Mum in a small voice. She returned Dad's hand squeeze. But the faraway look in Mum's eyes made me wonder if there was something more. Maybe it would be hard for her to go back after being away for so long. I know she'd found it hard to settle there as a teenager, and I sometimes got the sense that she felt guilty for wanting to move back to England, and that it was painful that my grandma had then left them to go back to live in Jamaica. Maybe there was a whisper of regret lingering somewhere inside of her at not going back sooner, or maybe she was hesitant to go back at all. I hadn't thought about it like that before. I'd been too busy bouncing off the walls with my own excitement. I hoped she'd have fun on this holiday – that's if she could free herself from Mum mode and start enjoying herself.

"But that was then, and this is now," said Dad with a broad beam. "We've got a lot of time to make up for!"

"Yes, and it's almost fifteen years ago since our very

special day," said Mum smiling sweetly and batting her eyelashes at Dad.

Dad's face suddenly dropped. His mouth contorted and his eyes twitched as if he'd been struck by a lightning bolt. He moved to say something, but then the Twinzies boinged into the room, legs made from springs, distracting everyone.

"Is dinner ready?" they asked in unison.

Dad exhaled with relief. He got to his feet hurriedly as if the Twinzies had rescued him from "a situation".

"Ooh, there's us getting distracted. Let's have no more of that. At your service. Dinner coming right up!" Dad almost fell over the coffee table in his hurry to leave the room.

But I hadn't forgotten that "I'm in big trouble" mashed-up contorted look on his face. What was up with Dad?

3

FRIENDS

Maybe it was all the talk of having no regrets, because the next day, Mum took a break from nagging me about organizing myself for our trip and let me spend Saturday afternoon over at Evie's house along with my best friends Charley and Arun.

I'm glad Mum let me go; I wanted to say a proper goodbye. By the time I'd be back from Jamaica, I'd barely have a chance to spend any more time with my friends before we all headed off to secondary school to be proper grown-up kids, wearing blazers and ties, carrying calculators, and doing other high-schooly stuff.

This felt like the last proper "before high school"

chance for us to hang out.

It was a hot day. If only Mum and Dad had had this kind of weather when they'd been on their soggy honeymoon.

I lay helplessly in Evie's garden hammock, like a crab flipped onto its back, floundering and unable to rescue myself, while still pondering what was up with Dad. Every way I had tried to twist and turn, I just couldn't get comfortable. There was no escape from the pulsating heat that made my whole body, from head to toe, feel like it was on fire.

I flopped one arm limply from the side of the hammock, finally giving up my fight.

"Anyone would think we were in the Sahara Desert, not in England," said Charley, draining the last bit of water from her glass. "Even the water is as warm as a cup of tea. The air is so still, as if there isn't any air left."

"Muggy, it's very muggy," announced Evie, as if she was a weather presenter, telling us the day's forecast. She had commandeered the shadiest spot in the garden, lying regally on a polka-dot patterned picnic blanket, underneath a leafy tree. I couldn't blame her for bagging the best spot. After all, it was her house.

"If it's as hot as this in England, it must be like a furnace in Jamaica," said Charley, her blue eyes popping out from the rim of her sun hat.

I sat up, leaning back on my elbows. I hadn't thought of that. After my experience of such a sweltering day in England, I wasn't sure I was ready for that kind of fire.

"Actually, I've been to many places in the world," crowed Evie. "The Caribbean is known for its lovely breezes, especially when you're near the sea."

"Oh, thanks, Evie," I said, appreciating her soothing, breezy words — and humble brag at the same time.

"Just watch out for the mosquitoes, they can bite HARD. Ouch!" she added, rubbing her arm, just to rub in the point.

A vision popped into my mind of giant mosquitoes, with sharp vampire fangs, out for my blood. I scrunched up my face and rubbed at my own arm as if the mosquitoes

were already attacking me.

"Pay no attention to me, I'm chatting too much. You'll be fine," said Evie, probably sensing my terror at the prospect of being eaten alive.

"Well, I think it's going to be scorching in India, too," said Arun, casually. Charley nodded and tried to drain more non-existent water from her empty glass.

"But you know what I do when I'm feeling hot under the collar? I just put on my shades and BE COOL." Arun took out his sunglasses from his shirt pocket, put them on and then double shuffled his eyebrows.

We all giggled so much that I lost balance and the hammock finally released me from captivity. I tipped out of it, my arms and legs sprawling everywhere as I rolled onto the grassy lawn, which made us all laugh even harder.

Everyone had plans for the rest of the summer holidays. Arun would be flying to India for his cousin's wedding, Charley would be going to Ireland with her family to visit relatives for a week, and Evie and her family were going on some kind of cruise. I couldn't keep up with her glamorous holidays.

I was glad that we all had something to look forward to. Not all summer holidays had been like this one, but the thought of being away from my friends also made my head throb. It wasn't just that we'd be going our separate ways for the rest of the six weeks' holiday that was making me feel on edge. It was the burning realization — which wasn't just because of the hot day — that I wouldn't be going to the same secondary school as any of them.

Arun had won a scholarship to the School of Music and Dramatic Arts — a school he desperately wanted to go to. Evie and Charley would be going to Greenhill Academy, and I had a place at Beeches Grammar School. Both Evie and I had sat the grammar school test, but she had just missed out on a place. My parents had put the grammar school down as my first choice and, as I'd achieved a high enough mark, that's the place I'd got.

Old worries that I'd pushed to the bottom of my stomach began to resurface, now that primary school was over and high school was around the corner. I'd written my stirred-up fears in my No Worries notebook, where I write down all the things I'm scared and worried about.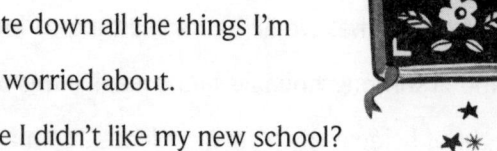

Suppose I didn't like my new school?

Suppose the work was too hard for me?

Could I really get to school on the bus by myself? (Having your parents drive you to school wouldn't seem very cool or grown-up, would it? Maybe they could take me just for the first week and drop me off around the corner?)

I'd have to make new friends. Could I really start over with a whole bunch of new people? No one else from Beeches Primary was going to my new school. And I'd missed my transition days in the summer term because I'd been sick with a tummy bug. Suppose everyone had started making new friends without me?

I was dead jealous to hear Evie and Charley speaking about meeting their form tutors and the things they'd be doing without me. My heart tightened into a giant knot at the thought.

I was scared of everything changing.

I swallowed down a little gulp. As much as I wanted to go on our dream holiday, this felt like the last days of being with my best friends, before everything changed for good.

4

CRYSTAL CLEAR

Thoughts of being a Sunny No-Mates filled my mind that afternoon, stinging like a swarm of wasps (or mosquitoes). But when I got back home from Evie's, I had something else to think about. I'd finally found out what was up with Dad. Let's just say, things became crystal clear.

It would be my parents' wedding anniversary while we were on holiday and Dad had forgotten about it.

Dad was pacing up and down the living room, rubbing his bald head while telling Auntie Sharon his sorry tale.

"I've only gone and forgotten about one of the most important days of our ENTIRE lives, haven't I? And it's a special anniversary, too. Fifteen WHOLE years." Dad paced up and down a bit more. "It's just that we've all been carried away with holiday fever — and Cheryl's constant cleaning to make sure the house is spick and span before we leave is quite distracting." Dad mopped at his brow as if he really had caught a fever.

"Ah, Tone, with the wonders of the internet and my cash overload, order anything you want. KERCHING!" encouraged Auntie Sharon.

"Well, I've been thinking," said Dad, his brow now creasing with all the thinking. "Fifteen years marks a crystal anniversary; I could buy Cheryl a lovely gift, like a vase or a bowl. But somehow that doesn't feel like it will quite cut it. I'm not being funny; fifteen years is a long time—"

"Yes, some might say a life sentence," interrupted Auntie Sharon, nodding thoughtfully.

Dad glossed over the "helpful" comment. "What I was going to say is, fifteen years is a long time, so I would like to do something special. Maybe…"

Dad paused and paced again.

"Yes, Dad? Tell us," I urged. I was dying to know about

the idea brewing in his furrowed head and, also, to stop him in his tracks before he wore out the living room rug with all the pacing.

"No, I can't, it's too outrageous!"

Dad piqued Auntie Sharon's interest. "Are you kidding me? OUTRAGEOUS should be my middle name, spelled in capital letters. Tell me more." Auntie Sharon licked her lips in anticipation.

"Well…" said Dad, lowering his voice to a whisper. "I was wondering, could we potentially organize a ceremony? A renewal of our wedding vows while we're over in Jamaica." Dad smiled. "I'm daydreaming about a sun-soaked celebration to make up for our rainy-days honeymoon. And also, because summer last year was so tough, what with Bobby passing away. I'd like to do something extra, extra special."

Auntie Sharon clapped one hand over her mouth to stop herself from screaming.

Dad's face fell. "It's a terrible idea, I knew it."

"TERRIBLE IDEA?" shouted Auntie Sharon, before hushing herself so that Mum wouldn't overhear. "I didn't know you had it in you, Tone. A second wedding? It's the best idea you've EVER had! And we're here for it. Aren't we, Sunshine?"

Were we here for it? I was the child in the room, yet Dad and Auntie Sharon started jumping up and down like excited little kids who'd eaten too much jelly and ice cream. We were going on holiday in less than forty-eight hours' time. How were we supposed to organize a wedding? Maybe it's because I was still feeling glum with my worries about secondary school and missing my friends, but someone had to give the grown-ups a reality check. Even though what Dad had said was just the nicest thing.

"Weddings take time to arrange, don't they? I'm sure godmother Patsy said she'd planned hers over the space of three WHOLE years. And what about wedding guests? Our friends and family here? Godmother Patsy and Mrs Turner—"

"Oh, don't worry about the finer details, we'll work it out," insisted Auntie Sharon, cutting me off mid-sentence. Her face glistened with mischief. "Besides, I'm sure Mrs Turner can fly over on her broomstick."

"SHARON!" exclaimed Dad. My Auntie Sharon and our neighbour Mrs Turner have a bit of a love/hate thing going on. Auntie Sharon thinks Mrs Turner has her eyes "too fixed on other people's business". To be fair, Auntie Sharon has a point.

"Ah, I'm only joking, Tone. Look, Sunny, I'm not talking about a big SHEBANG of a second wedding. I'm thinking we'll have a simple, understated affair."

"Simple" and "understated" aren't words you typically associate with my Auntie Sharon.

"Listen, yeah," continued Auntie Sharon, with her determined voice switched on. "You're right. Arranging a wedding so quickly, while on holiday, is a tall order for an ordinary person...but I ain't no ordinary person."

Dad and I both bobbed our heads up and down like those toy nodding dogs you sometimes see in people's cars. She wasn't wrong — there isn't anyone quite like Auntie Sharon.

"Let's give it a go, eh?" Auntie Sharon gave me an encouraging hug, which warmed me up to the idea. A bit.

"That's my girl." She beamed radiantly, but then her

smile dimmed. "Though you know what Cheryl's like. If she catches wind of this, she'll put out the fire faster than rain on bonfire night. NOT A WORD to anyone else in this family. Let's make this a **SURPRISEALICIOUS** secret for Cheryl."

I couldn't quite keep up with what we were getting ourselves into. The sudden holiday wedding, which we had to arrange in, surely, a record-breaking amount of time, was now also a **SURPRISEALICIOUS** secret. This was going to be IMPOSSIBLE to keep from Mum. She has hearing that would make a colony of bats jealous. No doubt her supersonic ears would suss this out in a nanosecond.

But then I looked up at the hopeful look on Dad's face and my heart melted. I gave him a reassuring smile and a thumbs up.

It was time for me to stop being the best resident of Moping Town if I was going to help Dad pull off the surprise wedding vows' renewal ceremony for Mum. But how could we keep it a secret from her? The answer to that question turned out to be, with great difficulty.

5

PINK FLAMINGO

Mum calling my name from upstairs jolted all of us out of the excitement.

I found her in the Twinzies' bedroom, wrestling a beach ball from Peter.

"But pleeeeeeasssseee, Mum," Peter pleaded. "There's no way they'll see the ball on the plane if I wear a jumper and hide it there."

"And pleeeeeasssseee, let me bring Betty the Bat as well as Brown Bunny," whined Lena. "They're best friends. If I leave Betty behind, she'll be lonely."

Mum put one hand out towards the Twinzies, as if she was a lollipop lady stopping traffic. "Nope. I'm sorry.

There's no more room in the suitcase. I'm sure Betty will be just fine. And, Peter, NO hiding things up jumpers." Mum flopped down onto the bed in a flummox.

"It's an open and shut case," I said, from the doorway, laughing to myself at my brilliant joke.

"You may laugh, Sunshine Simpson, but I'll be doing a spot check of your suitcase, once I've finished in here with the twins. So, I expect yours to be an open and shut case, too."

"On it, Mum!" I shouted as I bolted to my room.

I looked down at my suitcase. Apart from the toiletries, sandals and underwear that Mum had already packed, there was nothing else in it. There was only one thing I could do – PANIC PACK.

I started from scratch, emptying what was already in the suitcase onto my bed, to make a fresh start. How much do you pack for three weeks' holiday? Who knew? Well, Mum did, but I'd insisted I could do this on my own, and I didn't want to prove myself wrong and her right.

I hurriedly dumped the contents of a drawer filled with all my T-shirts into the case. I would probably need all of those, along with all my shorts, most of my trousers, four jumpers (just in case), three caps and a raincoat — as sometimes there can be short, sharp heavy showers in Jamica. I'd done the research.

I then added my desk globe (as a memory to take with me from home) and a pink flamingo float for the hotel's pool, that I'd kept in the corner of my room since our holiday in Devon. The pink flamingo floated precariously on top of the pile of clothes. And that's when I realized, I still needed to add the sandals, toiletry bag and underwear that I'd unpacked minutes earlier. Stacking those on top of the flamingo's long neck, I looked up at the Everest-high suitcase mountain. This wasn't working.

"Uh-oh, Sunny's in trouble!" I heard two voices sing from behind me. Peter and Lena were giggling.

"Help!" I pleaded.

"What's in it for us?" asked Peter.

I twisted my face in disgust that my brother and sister would take advantage of their own flesh and blood's perilous situation, but I was in no position to argue. "I'll buy ALL your ice creams at the hotel," I told them.

The Twinzies' faces lit up.

"Deal!"

I didn't mention that an all-inclusive holiday meant that everything we ate at the hotel would be free, including the ice cream. I know it was wrong, but these were desperate times.

"Quick! Both of you sit on the suitcase. I might be able to zip it up if you squash it down with your bums."

The Twinzies looked at each other with creased lips, doubting my rubbish plan.

"Well, have you got any better ideas?" I snapped. "Chocolate ice cream is slipping through your fingers by the second."

The Twinzies said no more and clambered up the side of the teetering mountain.

"Move your legs out of the way, will you, Lena? I can't get the zip round — and Peter STOP MOVING. You're worse than a wriggling worm."

"Hey!" shouted Peter, losing his balance, and promptly falling backwards onto the bed, but not before swinging his arm out and propelling Lena to the floor with a thud. Luckily, she landed on my fluffy rug.

Mum hurtled into the room.

"KARIS SUNSHINE SIMPSON!" she shouted, using my full name, in capital letters and italics, for extra oomph, which meant I was in trouble.

As it turned out, I ended up not so much in shouty trouble, it was more like *"I'm so disappointed in you, Sunshine"* sort of trouble, which always makes me feel much worse.

Mum sighed as she helped me fold clothes neatly and tidily into the case. (We had to lose the globe and pink flamingo float, sadly.)

"Sorry, Mum."

"Sunshine, now you're getting older and on the way to

BIG school, you'll need to be more organized. You'll have to make sure you have your school bag packed with all the right equipment and that you have clean uniform out every school night. It's all about discipline. And then when you eventually leave school, you'll be faced with real-world things to organize, so packing a suitcase may seem like a small thing, but this is all good prep. Life skills."

Now, I was sighing (inwardly). Talk about killing the holiday mood. Why do grown-ups always have to talk about preparing for the real world? Couldn't I just enjoy being eleven and worry about the real world later? And all this talk about being ready for school was making my insides curdle. I didn't like my new purple school uniform and the blazer felt too boxy and heavy. And don't even get me started on the tie. Every time I practised tying the stupid thing, it felt like it was a snake coiling around my neck suffocating me. Mum said that "most uniforms feel like that when they're new and just need getting used to...

and purple is a very regal colour". Well, if I wanted to be regal, I'd go to school in a castle. Pff!

Mum must have sensed the dip in my mood. "Look, I'm sorry, Sunny. I don't mean to sound like such a grumpy pants. It's my fault. I should have done this myself."

Which just made me feel even worse. (And I was going to ignore the fact she'd just used the words "grumpy pants" in a sentence.)

Mum continued to ramble on. "I am an organizer. That's what I do. It's fine. And I like it — mostly." She smiled. "Your poor dad hasn't even remembered our wedding anniversary, bless him. He won't, of course, if I don't remind him directly, which I won't. But it's fine, because I am the planner in this here town and I'm proud of it — so that's absolutely fine."

How many times had Mum used the word "fine" in the last minute? I think this meant she didn't feel fine at all.

She smiled wearily.

I wanted to tell her the truth. Yes, she was the best organizer in the family. Even better than Dad with all the spreadsheets he loved to use. Mum knew what to do in any situation, from a toilet brush getting stuck in the loo (don't ask) to a finger trapped in a door. She was multi-skilled. But this was her time to shine, sit back and enjoy her holiday. (And stop being such a bossy boots organizer — hopefully.) Yes, Dad did forget about their wedding anniversary at first, but now he had remembered, and he was planning the best anniversary gift **EVER**. But it was a secret.

"Don't you just ever want to have some fun?" I asked her in all seriousness.

Mum looked at me and did her favourite "I'm a little teapot" hands on hips move. "Sunny, I don't mean to be funny, but I don't have time to have fun. I'm too busy being Mum and getting you lot sorted."

I didn't know whether to feel insulted or a bit sorry for her. What it did give me was the added determination to pull this surprise second wedding off. My chance to show Mum that I could organize something too. Even if it wasn't my own suitcase.

PAINTED STONES

Later on that evening, I started feeling all wobbly again about the thought of high school and planning the surprise wedding. Could we really do it? Could *I* really do it? Any of it? It was obvious Mum thought I had absolutely ZERO chance of organizing myself for anything.

To settle myself, I went to my most favourite place in the world — Grandad Bobby's old bedroom.

I've always wanted to travel the world, but this house, particularly Grandad's room, makes me feel safe, protected — and the thought of leaving its four walls and crevices and corners suddenly made me feel a little unsteady.

Grandad's shelves still had his old knick-knacks on them. I smiled as I fixed my eyes on a couple of small stones on the shelf above his bed.

Grandad would always find a way to keep me entertained. We'd been for a treasure hunt around our back garden, years ago when I was six or so. I'd found two oval stones, close to the back fence. I liked them because they were as smooth and cool to touch as silk.

"What a find!" Grandad had said, holding the stones up to the sky and examining them as if I'd found gold. Really, they weren't that special. One stone was a dusty brown and the other a cloudy-day grey, but Grandad only saw treasure.

"We'll clean these up good and then paint them," he'd said. And that's exactly what we'd done that afternoon.

Grandad painted the brown stone in the colours of the Jamaican flag, black, gold and green and I'd painted a bright yellow sun, with streaking rays, onto the grey stone. Grandad had kept the stones on his shelf ever since. They still looked as good as the day we painted them. I picked up both stones, holding them in my hands,

oh so carefully, treating them as if they were rare gems, keeping the cherished memory of that day with Grandad cradled tightly in the palm of my hand.

Grandad said that the oval shape and the vivid colours of the painted Jamaican stone reminded him of a special mango tree in his garden at Old Farm that he and his sister, Violet, used to climb to pick the juicy mangoes. They would then climb down, sit underneath the tree, peel the golden mangoes with their fingers and teeth, and eat until they had bellyaches.

"All kinds of mangoes grow in Jamaica, but those are my favourite of all – the Number 11 mango," Grandad had said. "To me, it is the most royal of mangoes. They were my sister's favourites too. Do you know, my sister Violet was little, mischievous, and loved her own way. One day when I was doing a job for my dad on the other side of the field, I left her at the tree. 'Sit underneath it,' I told her, 'DO NOT CLIMB IT without me, Vi!' She didn't listen and she went up that tree — and 'if you can't hear yuh will feel', as we say in Jamaica. Well, I have a memory of running over to her and time moving in slow motion, stopping me from getting there on time as I watched her fall, streaking out of the sky like a shooting star."

"And what happened to her, Grandad?" I'd shrieked. "Did she break her head?"

"Well, no, Sunshine, I'm glad it wasn't so drastic, but she did break her arm, which was bad enough. And straight after it healed, she was back up in that tree again. There was no keeping her down. She certainly had courage. When she was scared, she beat down the fear by doing whatever it was anyway. But I made her swear an oath that she wouldn't climb that tree again without me. 'Cross my heart,' she told me. I had nightmares about that fall for years and I swore I'd never leave her again. But, of course, I did leave her when I came to England."

I'd noticed a cloudy, faraway look in Grandad's eyes.

"Did you wish you'd stayed with your sister to look after her in Jamaica?"

"Well, at the time, coming over to England was hard

for me. I didn't want to leave my family, but I needed to come and make money to send back home for the upkeep of the farm. But God sent me new little chicks to look after in the end. And I wouldn't have it any other way."

I remember grabbing Grandad around his tummy then and giving him a big hug. He laughed that big booming laugh of his and patted me on the head. Courage. That's what Grandad had helped me to have, just like his sister, Vi. Did I imagine it, or was there a pulsating heat coming from the stones, running through my fingers, into my arms and then filling my whole body with a warm glow?

"You, okay, baby girl?" I heard a voice call from behind me, pulling me from my memories. It was Dad standing at the bedroom door.

"Yes, Dad, I'm good, thanks." I smiled.

"Ready to go and organize a rock and roll wedding?" Dad did an air-guitar move (oh my poor dad, I think he is beyond help). He grimaced and then smiled a goofy smile at me.

I giggled. "Yes... I think I am ready." I opened my hand and carefully placed the stones back onto the shelf.

"That's my girl. It'll take the two of us to rein in your Auntie Sharon."

I gave him a double thumbs up. "We're the team to do it," I rallied.

And I meant it.

I stayed up late that evening having a secret group video call with Charley, Arun and Evie. Auntie Sharon said that no one in the family could know about the plans for the surprise wedding, so technically, I figured, there was no harm in telling my friends.

I spoke in hushed tones in case Mum was hovering somewhere nearby listening in, like she usually did to make sure we were having "appropriate conversations" — or more likely she'd throw me off the phone completely as it was so late in the evening. I swear there are more rules, curfews and locks on my phone than an actual prison.

"That is AWESOME," said Arun. "One day they'll turn your mum and dad's Wedding Part Two into a film. It's SO Hollywood!"

"Um… I guess." Even on our call, Arun was chatting while practising pirouettes, which, I must admit, was making me a little dizzy with all the whirling.

"Oh wow! Your mum's such a super-sleuth though, isn't she? How will you keep it a secret?" asked Charley.

"Good question," I replied. "With great difficulty, probably, but I'll give it my best shot, until it kills me. Unless Mum kills us first — which might happen if Auntie Sharon gets carried away with everything." I swallowed hard at the thought of what kind of wedding Auntie Sharon might unleash onto the universe.

"Do you remember when I came over to yours after school and we decided to make a quick sneaky snack before tea while your mum was upstairs, and then she caught us? Your mum ran down and burst into the kitchen because she thought she could smell burning toast!" said Charley.

"What's wrong with that?" asked Evie.

"We hadn't even put the bread into the toaster yet — and we'd shut the kitchen door tightly and everything!" said Charley, shaking her head, still in disbelief at the memory.

"I think my mum's superpowers are seeing through doors and walls and being one step ahead of time." I sighed.

"Well, it sounds like it's not going to be easy," chuckled Evie. "But my dad always says the best things never are."

I gave Evie a hopeful nod.

"It sounds like so much fun! I wish we could help you organize it," said Arun.

"But we're only a phone call away. ALWAYS and FOREVER," cheered Charley.

"You can do it!" cried Evie.

"Can I? I mean…thanks. Or I'll just make Mum walk around with headphones and a blindfold on for three weeks."

We all laughed.

I'd miss my friends. A lot.

Mum popped her head around the door just as I'd finished the call. "Everything all right, Sunny? I thought I heard voices."

I smiled. What did I say about Mum's superpowers? "Everything's good, Mum. Just really excited for the holiday."

Mum kissed me on the head. "A new adventure awaits," she said.

It did. For me and for her.

BETTY THE BAT

By the time Mum woke us up at FIVE O'CLOCK on Monday morning to make sure we were on time for our flight, I had dark circles under my eyes the size of the pink flamingo ring. I'd been tossing and turning so much in nervous anticipation for the trip that I felt like I'd barely slept.

After a final check of all the suitcases, Mum made the Twinzies and me sit down for breakfast. She didn't want to let any food go to waste, so there was practically a whole loaf of bread to eat our way through before we went on holiday.

Mum darted around us cleaning and disinfecting

everywhere, so the house would smell "nice and fresh" when we returned. I wouldn't have minded but she'd already cleaned the house from top to bottom twice that week — and how much of the scent of Forest Pine disinfectant does one house need?

As we were munching, Peter kept glancing at the kitchen clock.

"Has time stood still?" he asked.

"Ha! If only," said Mum. "But at least we've had time to have a good breakfast. You all just need to get dressed. The taxi's not due for another forty-five minutes." Mum let out a sigh of relief and sipped at her cup of tea.

"But the clock's been saying the same time for an AWFULLY long time," said Peter.

Mum swung round to check the clock, spilling her cup of tea onto her freshly mopped floor. "Where's my phone?" she shouted. "I need to check the time!" Then Mum remembered about her own rule that we're not allowed phones at the kitchen table as "it interferes with family time". So, she clambered onto a chair, took the clock off the wall and put it to her ear.

Her eyes virtually popped out of her head on stalks. "THE CLOCK'S STOPPED!" she yelled.

There was a ring at the doorbell. Dad hurried from the breakfast table to answer it.

"THE TAXI'S HERE!" Dad was yelling now too.

Suddenly, there was chaos.

Mum flung the Twinzies and me upstairs to brush our teeth and to dress and Dad started throwing suitcases into the boot of the taxi.

Peter came downstairs in a T-shirt and pyjama bottoms and was promptly marched back upstairs by Mum, to put his trousers on.

I found myself slipping into Grandad's room.

"Sunny, hurry up, we're LATE!" shouted Mum.

"I'll be down in a minute, just grabbing my bag."

In all the chaos, I still needed to say goodbye to Grandad. I know that probably sounds silly, but I'd never been so far away from home before, from Grandad's things. I needed the moment. I needed calm.

"Bye, Grandad's room, I'll be back soon," I whispered. I ran my fingers over all of Grandad Bobby's special treasures. I wished he was coming with us.

I closed one fist tightly around the most special treasure of all, and then walked backwards out of the room, closing the door gently with my other hand. I took a deep breath. I was ready to roll.

Our neighbour, Mrs Turner, came out onto the pavement and talked Mum and Dad's ears off before they launched themselves into the taxi. Mrs Turner wafted a white handkerchief at us to wave goodbye. Isn't waving something white meant to mean surrender? I should have taken it as a sign of things to come.

"Have we got everything?" asked Mum as we waved back at Mrs Turner and the taxi drove towards the end of our road. "It feels like we're missing something."

"Everything's under control. Passports. Check. Suitcases. Check. I've even remembered to pack my toothbrush," said Dad, grinning from the front seat.

Mum smiled and exhaled.

I was squished into the middle seat behind Dad, in between Peter and Mum. Peter always gets to sit next to the window, because he insists he gets car sick. Oof! Lena had managed to bagsy the best seat in the taxi. An individual seat right at the back, next to the boot. I swivelled round to see the satisfied grin on her face. But there was a problem. I turned back around, searching from left to right, and then investigated the front passenger seat where Dad was. There were no other seats in the car.

"Um, Mum...Dad," I said, after twisting behind me to double-check the seat at the back.

"Yes, Sunny?"

I didn't want to alarm them, so as calmly as possible I said, "Lena doesn't seem to be in the car."

The taxi screeched to a halt — and the driver reversed back down the road as if the taxi was powered by lightning.

We all ran to the front door, Dad fumbling the keys in his hurry to unlock it. Lena stood in the hallway, hugging her toy, looking lost. Talk about *Home Alone*!

"When you were talking to Mrs Turner I climbed out of the boot, over the suitcases, and went back upstairs to get Betty the Bat. I just couldn't leave her behind. But when we came down, you'd gone," said Lena, in a small voice.

Mum flung her hands to her mouth in shock at what — or should I say who — we'd almost left behind. "Fine. She can come! Let's get Betty the Bat strapped in, shall we? She's got a holiday waiting for her — if we ever get there. I hope you've packed her suncream!"

Lena grinned wildly.

Dad scooped Lena and Betty into his arms and gave them both raspberry squishy kisses, and then we all scooted back down the garden path and into the taxi.

The taxi driver shook his head and raised his eyes to the heavens.

We were finally off to the airport.

8

IRON BIRD

For the first time EVER, I was going to be travelling on an "iron bird". That's what my Grandad Bobby used to call an aeroplane. I could feel my insides glowing hotter than a jumbo jet's engine at the thought of flying to a land far, far away. I was nervous. Excited. Excitedly nervous. How did planes even stay up in the air? I decided this wasn't the best time to start pondering that particular mechanical miracle.

Dad, Mum, the Twinzies, Granny Cynthie, Grampie Clive (who we met up with at the airport) and I waited impatiently in the airport lobby for Auntie Sharon, her boyfriend Dennis and my cousin Daz to arrive. Then we spotted them. Well, we saw Auntie Sharon first. Dennis and Daz were travelling someway behind her, taking it in turns to push a giant trolley piled high with suitcases, most of them Auntie Sharon's. You could tell they were Auntie Sharon's cases because they had a matching leopard print pattern. In fact, as they approached, the suitcases almost resembled a leap of leopards stalking their way across the Serengeti.

"Watch the dry-land tourist," said Granny Cynthie as she surveyed Auntie Sharon's extravagant, head-turning outfit. Auntie Sharon was wearing a long, floral sundress, a large sun hat, golden strappy-heeled sandals and sunglasses that almost swallowed her face whole, as if she was already swaying through the tropical streets of Jamaica.

Dennis mopped at his sweating brow after the exertion of pushing Auntie Sharon's suitcases through the packed airport. Poor Dennis, he is so quiet and laid-back. Unlike Auntie Sharon.

"Greetings, family," Auntie Sharon called, waving merrily.

"What time do you call this?" asked Mum.

Auntie Sharon smiled widely. "JAMAICA time! What are we waiting for?"

Well, we'd been waiting for Auntie Sharon for ages, but Mum didn't have a chance to tell her off, because then Auntie Sharon started singing a jolly song called "Hooray, Hooray, it's a Holi-Holiday" and getting random people all around to join in. Mum had to pull her away after three rounds of the chorus to make sure we wouldn't miss our plane. Mum didn't want to take any more chances after our frantic morning rush.

"Why the hurry?" called Auntie Sharon. "No need to dash when you're travelling in style."

Auntie Sharon was right. Once we'd put our carry-on bags through security checks, we were all whizzed into the "premium" lounge, which was like a Santa's grotto for travellers, full of delicious, edible presents.

There was every kind of juice to drink – apple, orange, cranberry, tomato (EWW!), pineapple. And there were fizzy drinks galore. I had a glass of Coke, which, for once, Mum let me have – even though it was still only the morning.

And then I tried to sneak a glass of Fanta past her hawk eyes — but, of course, Mum caught me orange-handed. "Oh, go on then. We're on our holidays, after all." Mum beamed.

But perhaps the best bit of the airport — aside from the free food and drink — was that part of it was glass-fronted, which meant we could see the airfield below and all the planes on the runway that looked like they were about to take part in their own aeroplane Olympics. Big planes. Smaller planes. Each with colourful rudders that looked like they'd been dipped into paint pots.

Dad, the Twinzies and I glued our faces to the giant window, as if we were watching a TV show on a big screen. A TV show all about planes. Our heads followed one plane as it travelled swiftly down the runway and then soared into the sky like a mechanical eagle. Its little lights flashed like blinking stars. It really was an iron bird.

We let out breaths of astonishment — even Dad watched the plane rise in open-mouthed wonder.

"Whoa!" said Peter. "I want to fly one of those."

"Me too," said Lena.

"Me three," I said.

"Me four," said Dad.

"Psst…psst!"

I heard the sound but, at first, ignored it, my eyes still dazzled by the plane's climbing, clambering beauty. But the "pssting" persisted, until I finally looked over in the direction of where the sound was coming from. One of the airport's concrete pillars seemed to be talking to me. A diamond finger extended from behind the pillar and called me towards it. As if the pillar had arms.

I nudged Dad and we left the Twinzies to watch the plane as its huge frame became a smaller and smaller dot on the horizon.

"I have news!" cried Auntie Sharon, as she yanked us both behind the pillar. "We're in luck! I've found a venue for the nuptials."

Dad and I widened our eyes in excitement.

"The Grand Beach Hotel, where we're staying, offers wedding packages. They've had a last-minute cancellation. There's been a bit of DRAH-MA! A poor bride fell down a flight of stairs while she was practising a graceful descent at home in her wedding dress. She's broken her leg, which admittedly was unlucky for her. Sadly, that wedding's OFF OFF OFF, but, in a dramatic twist of fate, means that ours is ON ON ON."

"Oh," said Dad, rubbing his forehead. "That brings a whole new meaning to the term 'break a leg'."

"Doesn't it just," said Auntie Sharon, drily. "I do feel sorry for the poor bride, but 'what's gone bad in the morning, can't come good again in the evening', as my old dad used to say, so we better make the most of it. You're getting married on the 28th of August! The actual day of your crystal wedding anniversary. It's written in the stars."

I did a quick calculation in my head — that would be halfway through the third and last week of our holiday. At least that gave us extra time to arrange everything... but also even longer to keep the secret!

Auntie Sharon clapped her hands in delight. "Isn't it exhilarating? It's going to be a challenge, for sure, but challenge should be my second middle name — after outrageous. I'm ready. Are you two?"

Dad nodded eagerly, his eyes twinkling like the plane's lights. Rushed along on Auntie Sharon's wave of excitement, I didn't want to let the team down, so I nodded too.

"Winner, winner, chicken and rice and peas dinner," cackled Auntie Sharon. She stretched a reassuring arm around one of my shoulders. "Trust me, kid, you'll see nothing like this wedding EVER again."

Auntie Sharon always has a way of making the impossible seem possible. I swallowed down my doubts with a gulp. If we had Auntie Sharon's enthusiasm to bob us along then I suppose Dad's wedding dream could turn into a reality. And it was lovely that the ceremony would be on Mum and Dad's anniversary itself.

"Tony, this is going to be *the* WEDDING OF THE YEAR. You're going to get married again in style!" said Auntie Sharon.

"Why is Dad getting married again?" asked Lena in horror.

"You're already married to Mummy!" cried Peter.

Uh-oh! We'd been busted by the Twinzies. We had no choice but to let them in on the secret before they got confused and blabbed to Mum that Dad was getting married again to someone else.

"You can help us by keeping Mum distracted," I suggested, once we'd told them the truth. "If anyone can keep Mum occupied for twenty-four hours a day, it's you two."

The Twinzies looked thoroughly insulted, but huddled in a secret scrum anyway, whispering to each other.

"What's in it for us?" said Lena. "Can Brown Bunny and Betty the Bat come to the wedding too?"

Dad, Auntie Sharon and I looked at each other. Was that all they were asking for? I thought the Twinzies would be getting hush money out of this situation, at least. Jamaican and American dollars to spend on the trip. What a wasted opportunity.

"Um, sure," I agreed.

"And ice cream — you'd already promised us LOTS!" said Peter.

"You can have as much ice cream as you like!" I told him. Dad frowned but said nothing. He knew what was best for him.

Lena and Peter went back into their huddle.

"OKAY! What's the code?" asked Peter, once they'd finished in their scrum.

"Huh?"

"You know, the code? The sign? Whenever you want us to distract Mum, we need to know when to strike. You can't leave this to chance," said Lena, like a professional distractor.

"Oh." I thought about it for a moment. "How about when you see me pat my head, you jump into action?" I patted my head three times and Auntie Sharon and Dad did the same. We all laughed at how silly we must have looked. The Twinzies didn't seem impressed, but there was no time to think of anything different.

Mum had been to the airport's toilets, but I glimpsed her striding over. She'd probably sensed with her laser superpowers that there was something going on. I patted my head three times.

The Twinzies didn't hesitate. They swung round and into action, pulling Mum back in the direction of the toilets.

Maybe they'd turn out to be our best assets? Twinzies — welcome aboard!

9

FIRST CLASS

If I'd thought the airport was thrilling, it didn't compare to what was about to come next.

We walked along a big, concertinaed bridge, which sounded like we'd been caught in a very windy tunnel as we travelled along it. We were astronauts about to step onto the moon, taking one small step for humans and a giant leap for humankind. When we reached the plane's door, a smiley cabin crew member welcomed us on board.

"It's our first time on a plane," I heard myself gabbling about the Twinzies and myself.

The cabin crew member's smile stretched to a grin. "And you couldn't be going to a better destination. I hope you have the time of your lives. You're certainly travelling in style." He gestured for us to go to the left side of the plane.

The cabin crew member was right. I threw my hands to my mouth to stop myself from squealing. Did all planes look like this on the inside?

Each of us had our own dedicated areas like little space pods, with a TV, comfy, large chair, fluffy blanket, mini-fridge and our own cupboards.

I took a few photos to send to Arun, Charley and Evie as I had done in the airport lounge.

"I was born for first-class service," said Auntie Sharon, sighing happily.

"And you deserve it," said Dennis, squeezing Auntie Sharon's hand, in a move that was sweet but also as soppy as a wet towel. Dennis did look a bit green in his face though.

Dennis is a driving instructor; he'd been looking very nervous about travelling on something where he wasn't in control of the brakes.

"You feeling all right, Mr Snuggles?" Auntie Sharon

cooed at him, as if she was a pigeon.

Mr Snuggles nodded weakly. "Nothing dry land won't cure, my little Shazzy Bear."

YUCK! I made a mental note to stop Auntie Sharon from writing Mum and Dad's wedding vows. The last thing I wanted to hear was any more romantic slush. Pass the sick bag! At least every aeroplane seat has one!

Mum wasn't so sure about the Twinzies and me having our own individual areas. She spent most of her time pacing up and down between us and fussing to see whether we were all right. She sat close to the Twinzies to keep an eye on them, and I was in a seat next to Dad.

Dad and I both leaned forward peeking at each other at the same time from beyond our little areas. We grinned wildly and gave each other a double thumbs up. "We're like two peas in a pod," said Dad excitedly. Sometimes I think my dad is a kid in an adult's body. But I wouldn't have him any other way.

As the plane's engines began to whir, the cabin crew member made sure we were all strapped in tightly. I heard myself gulp.

We were off…

Travelling along the runway, slow at first, and then faster and faster; breathless. My stomach turned over as the plane took off into the air, climbing, climbing…

My ears popped. A fuzzy dullness filled the space between my ears and my brain, as if someone had stuck fingers in my ears and wouldn't take them out. I gripped my seat in terror, holding on so tightly, I was scared I'd pierce a hole through it. But as the plane found its way, jolting and bumping, eventually becoming level, I felt my fears subside. My ears popped back to life after a few minutes, and I relaxed. We were a flying hotel in the sky.

As the iron bird flew over the rooftops of houses, farms and fields, England became a tiny dot as small as a pinprick. Once the country had finally disappeared, dissolving into sky and clouds, I explored my pod. The space was incredible. Even when stretching out my long legs, there was plenty of room to spare. And there were so many buttons to push. One button adjusted the lights from dim to bright. Another made the lights change colour, as if we were in a disco in the clouds. I pressed the button at the side of my chair; the seat sailed backwards to a horizontal position. A comfy bed! I pushed another button that brought me back up to vertical. It was a dentist's chair, I thought, without the dentist and the horrible rinsing mouthwash. But as comfortable as this chair-bed was, I wasn't ready for a nap. There was far too much to explore.

I pulled open the small cupboard at the side of my chair. A mini wardrobe slid out, with fluffy slippers, socks, an eye mask, lovely-smelling toiletries, and the softest, smoothest pyjamas inside. I even had a pair of binoculars and noise-cancelling headphones.

The cabin crew member, Mark, who had greeted us at the door, offered us all little boxes filled with chocolates. I almost scoffed the whole lot in one go. One was pure silky chocolate, another oozed with caramel, a third crunched with delicious ground almonds. I left the last one – a chocolate truffle shaped like a present and wrapped in golden foil – wanting to savour it later. So, I had a glass of fizzy apple juice instead. Mark handed me a champagne flute to drink from.

"If you're going to fly in style, why not drink in style?" Mark said with a grin.

I pursed my lips around the slim glass and inhaled, sucking the gassy bubbles up my nose like a noisy vacuum cleaner. I coughed, spluttered and giggled. Surely this was better than real champagne. I'd never had a drink that tasted so good. This was the life. I was buzzing (probably from all the sugar).

Before I settled back in my comfy bed seat to watch TV, I took out my Things and Places of Interest notebook and turned my mind to my parents' wedding vows' ceremony.

Dad had promised Mum he'd leave his laptop at home and have a proper relaxing break. So, because Dad wouldn't have access to his beloved spreadsheets on holiday, I'd told him we could make a list of what we'd need for the wedding in my notebook. I was always jotting things down in it, so hopefully Mum wouldn't be suspicious.

According to everything I'd read online about

organizing a wedding vows' renewal ceremony, I had to "visualize" exactly how I wanted it to be. Hmm... I've only ever been to one wedding. I was a bridesmaid for Mum's best friend, my godmother Patsy. My lasting memory of that wedding was wearing a big puffed-out bridesmaid's dress that looked like I was wearing an air balloon and it got stuck in my pants after I'd been to the toilet. Frills should be illegal as far as I'm concerned. Why would you make dresses with so much material? Anyway, I would just have to "un-visualize" that terrible memory — and remember this day wasn't about me, it was about Mum and Dad.

I rubbed at my temples and focused on the wedding "Things to Do" list I'd already started at home, jotting down a few more things on the plane. Mum thought I needed to be more organized, so I was going to work very hard to be the new organized me:

1. **A wedding venue.** We'd already managed to tick that one off the list thanks to Auntie Sharon. I'd seen pictures of the Grand Beach Hotel online, and it looked

spectacular. We'd have to check where they held the ceremony when we got there. Would we have the wedding inside or outside in the hotel's pretty gardens or even on the sandy beach? Or better still at one of the hotel's SIX swimming pools!

2. **Speak to the wedding planner.** Auntie Sharon said we'd need to meet with a lady called Miss Babette, so she could help us to design the wedding of Mum and Dad's dreams.

3. Dad would need to show **important legal papers** which would mean that Mum and Dad could go ahead with the renewal of their marriage vows. I mean, they are already properly married, so I didn't know why this was so important, but big people seem to like unnecessary paperwork. I'd have to trust Dad would be grown-up enough to do that boring bit by himself.

4. **Wedding vows.** Dad would have to make up something syrupy to say to Mum on the day. ~~Auntie Sharon to write Mum's vows.~~ Shazzy Bear and Mr Snuggles would NOT be allowed anywhere near Mum's vows. I'd just have to find something less sickly sweet for

Mum to say to Dad. Perhaps she could read the lyrics from a popular song that everyone would recognize? Something by Taylor Swift or Beyoncé? "Shake it Off"? "Crazy in Love"? Hmm... I needed to keep thinking about that one.

5. **The reception**. Food, music, cutlery, tablecloths, flowers! Mum likes things to be simple and straightforward. Would I be able to restrain Auntie Sharon, who likes things to be fancy and flashy?

6. **A guest list**. Who else would we invite apart from Lena's toys? I felt guilty that people like Mrs Turner and godmother Patsy wouldn't be there. And I felt a lump in my throat not to be able to share the special occasion with my own friends. And what about our Jamaican relatives? Would they be able to come at such short notice?

7. **CAKE!!!** The most important part of the day, surely? We needed a massive wedding cake to be the centrepiece. You can't have a party without cake!

I looked over my list. How on earth were we going to get all these things done in less than three weeks? Plus, I had a nagging feeling I'd forgotten something.

Once I'd done with the list, I ate a delicious meal of rice and peas, macaroni cheese and curried chicken, followed by banoffee pie, served to me at my seat by Mark.

"Can I help you with the washing-up?" I asked when I'd done eating. I felt bad that Mark was up and down the aisles catering for our every need.

He smiled at me. "Ha! Don't worry, I've got you covered."

I settled down with my noise-cancelling headphones on to watch TV as there was nothing much else to see out of the window now but sky.

I must have drifted off to sleep, because the next thing I remember is waking up, taking off the headphones, and yawning, as a familiar voice filled the air.

"We're approaching Jamaica, we're finally here!" At first, I thought it was Peter speaking in his overexcited *"I'm a boy who eats too many sweets"* voice.

But it was Dad.

He was suddenly next to me craning his head to look out of the window, with a smile as wide as the ocean below sweeping across his face.

As I turned to look out of the plane's tiny window, I saw it, too. **JAMAICA**.

I gasped at the sight.

What stretched out before me took my breath away. I whipped the binoculars out of the side-cupboard to take a closer look.

Shimmering blues and vibrant greens of sky, land and sea flooded my vision. I realized in that moment that this small island was bigger in my heart than I could ever have imagined. If it was this beautiful from above, as we glided through the air, what wonders did this new land hold for me down below?

Before we got off the plane, instead of keeping it for myself as I'd planned, I offered Mark the chocolate box that had the golden truffle in it. Seeing it now, I felt a bit silly and greedy that I'd demolished the rest. "I just wanted to say thank you for looking after us. I'm sorry I only left you one." We both looked at the paltry offering, sitting alone in the box like a solitary island.

"Well, that is truly kind. Thank you." Mark smiled, warmly. "I'll have it with a cup of tea, later. You certainly live up to your name, Sunshine. I've enjoyed having you as a special guest. Safe travels — and HAPPY HOLIDAY!"

I beamed. This was really it: the start of my Jamaican adventure, and I was so happy to be here.

10

MARINE BAY

The airport was decked out in black, gold and green bunting, as if we'd stepped into the middle of a Jamaican coronation, and we were the honoured guests.

Was this all a dream? We had left England at ten o'clock in the morning. Because of the five hours' time difference between England and Jamaica, and the ten-hour flight, my brain felt mushy. If we had still been in England, it would be seven o'clock in the evening, but now here we were in Jamaica at two o'clock in the afternoon.

The view as we stepped out of the airport's doors jolted me to my senses — the brightness was electrifyingly WOW. In front of us, swaying palm trees waved their branches, and beyond — as far as my eyes could see — lusciously green mountains stood proudly, as tall as skyscrapers.

I wondered whether this was how the early settlers from the Windrush generation felt as they walked down their ships' gangways and stepped into their new lives in Britain. New sights, new sounds, so much to take in. Their view would have been vastly different to what I was seeing now, of course. England, especially for those who arrived in coldest, darkest winter, must have been a shock to the system: cold, wet and grey. My grandparents said they thought all the clustered buildings with the smoke coming out of the chimneys were factories, and they were so shocked when they realized they were houses. But, as if telling the Windrush story in reverse, here I was seeing Jamaica in glorious technicolour.

The sun rose out of the ground, a shimmering heat filling every inch of our surroundings, as if saying **HELLO,**

WELCOME HOME – greeting us with a kiss and a warm hug. But the heat didn't feel stifling. A soothing breeze whipped across us. Evie had been right; the heat did feel different here.

We stuffed ourselves into a minibus taxi that the hotel had arranged to meet us.

The clustered palm trees waved their goodbyes as we left the airport, bowing their branches in the breeze. We were off to the Grand Beach Hotel!

The hotel was in an area called Marine Bay, so we took the highway. Trees and bushes popped out along the route; the line of green only broken up by houses. Most of these houses were one storey high and came in an assortment of gummy bear colours: mint green, sky blue, sunshine yellow, blazing red. Jewels dotted amidst the green landscape. There were also other buildings along the roadside resembling cabins. Dad said these were restaurants and shops.

Peter asked a question I'd been meaning to ask. "Will we get to meet Usain Bolt?"

"Well, Peter, even though Jamaica's known as a small

island, it's still quite a big place," said Dad, batting off the question with the speed of Usain Bolt himself.

"I hear he's a cousin of ours, you know," said Auntie Sharon, nodding her head enthusiastically.

"Sharon, you say we're related to every famous Jamaican!" Dad smiled.

Mum was looking out of the window, thoughtful and quiet, sunglasses covering her eyes. It must have been strange for her being back here after all these years.

"You okay, Chez?" Auntie Sharon asked Mum.

"Yes, I was just thinking, the country seems to have changed in so many ways, but in other ways feels the same. The roads are less bumpy than I remember them, which is good. Journeys used to feel like you were on a rollercoaster ride."

"Drink it in all in, Chez, the green, green grass of home! I hear that sometimes they shoot films on location at the Grand Beach Hotel too. Maybe we'll see some film stars while we're there?"

Mum and Auntie Sharon shared a smile. Mum loves films.

I think one of the reasons that Auntie Sharon was so desperate to pull off the surprise second wedding was so that Mum would have new, warmer memories of being in Jamaica. Auntie Sharon always seemed to love talking about Jamaica, but with Mum, it was different. She never wanted to talk about it. I wondered why she and Auntie Sharon had left all those years before. Why couldn't they settle down to live there?

Looking at Mum now, I was even more determined to help Auntie Sharon and Dad with this wild plan.

As we drew closer to Marine Bay, a raw freshness mixed with tangy saltiness filled our noses, and the scenery transformed. The vibrant greens of grass and trees, and the brightly coloured houses and shops, morphed into shades of aqua and turquoise.

The sea. **THE SEA**.

Foamy waves lapped invitingly, calling us closer.

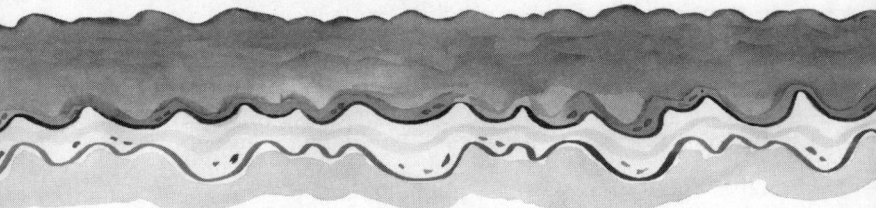

A white ship, tiered like a giant wedding cake, loomed into view. I chuckled to myself. If only I could arrange a cake as big as this ship for

Mum and Dad's 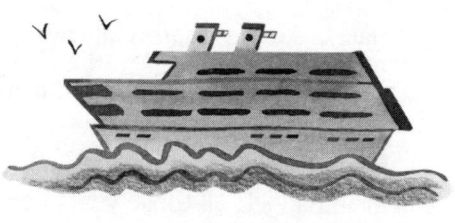 second wedding it would be the perfect centrepiece and we'd be eating slices for months.

The ocean liner, stacked with window upon window, looked like a thousand eyes were peering back at us. I wondered whether Evie's cruise ship would be this big. It was like a gigantic floating hotel in the ocean.

If the ocean liner was this enormous, then what would the Grand Beach Hotel be like? I couldn't wait to get there!

THE GRAND BEACH HOTEL

The Grand Beach Hotel rose majestically from the ground in shining white splendour.

The hotel swept around in a horseshoe shape and huddled close to a pretty, manicured garden, with a lawn so neat and tidy, it looked like it had been painted. Swaying palm trees sprung from the lawn; red and yellow flowers danced in the breeze, adding bursts of summery-bright colours; and a large hedge had been expertly cut and shaped into the words GRAND BEACH HOTEL. The impressive front garden was broken up by a pond, with a bubbling fountain at the centre. A bridge stretched from the garden across the pond to an arched pagoda. This was

magical — a perfect place for a fairy-tale wedding. I made a mental note to jot the pond and pagoda down as a number one hot spot for Mum and Dad's wedding vows' renewal ceremony. As a grown-up might say, "this had potential".

The hotel was equally magnificent inside. We walked into a large, covered lobby area, where white floor tiles glistened as if they'd been sprinkled with diamonds... Past the wicker chairs and tables, dotted around for people to sit and relax, our eyes trailed to something that made us stop and stare.

There were no windows or doors to separate the outside from the inside. Instead a glass balcony stretched from one side to the other, offering the most spectacular view of a golden sandy beach and an endless bright, blue ocean.

The Twinzies, Daz and I ran over to the balcony in

wide-eyed wonder, our mouths formed into an "o" shape to drink in what we were seeing.

The beach and the sea stretched on and on. It was as if we were looking at an artist's painting in the Birmingham Museum and Art Gallery or something. I was scared to blink, just in case, when opening my eyes again, the view would disappear, as if I'd made it all up.

The grown-ups wandered over to us, holding bright orange drinks with colourful paper umbrellas sticking out of them, that had been thrust into their hands to welcome them to the hotel. I don't think I've ever seen my parents so relaxed and happy. It really did feel like we were now on the holiday of a lifetime. Even my cousin, Daz, who is usually more laid-back than a deckchair, looked excited.

I took a selfie with the sea and the beach and the blue skies behind me and sent it to Charley, Arun and Evie. "Hello from beautiful Marine Bay!" I said gleefully in my message. I'd been taking and sending so many photos to Arun, Charley and Evie ever since I'd got to the airport at home in England, that my phone felt like it was on fire. But I hadn't received any messages back from them. Had my friends had enough of me? Was I showing off too much sending all these photos? Too smug? Too OTT?

I wrung my hands. I didn't want to lose my old friends, especially if I couldn't make new friends at my new school. I just didn't want to lose them FULL STOP, whether I had new friends or not. But what if our friendship slipped away when we were at our different schools?

Huh? I shook my head to chase away the sad thoughts. I couldn't think about that right now. I didn't want to spoil this special moment. Besides, I had a wedding to plan and a hotel bedroom to stake out.

Auntie Sharon and Dennis had their own room, and so did Mum and Dad. Here was the sting. Daz — because he's five years older than me at sixteen — got his own room too, while the Twinzies and I had to share with Grampie Clive and Granny Cynthie. I scrunched up my face in disappointment, but said nothing, as I didn't want Grampie and Granny to think that I didn't want to hang out with them. I mean, I did, just not so closely! But when we got to our room, not for the first time that day, my mouth hit the floor in astonishment. The Twinzies, Granny, Grampie and I were in the Superior Family Suite, which had TWO king-sized beds.

"Peter and Lena, you two will share a bed," said Granny Cynthie.

HUH? That was the final straw. There was **NO WAY** I was about to share the other bed with Granny and Grampie. A girl's got to have some dignity. Granny and Grampie must have seen the look on my face because both started giggling.

"It's quite all right, Sunshine. We aren't going to cramp your style." Grampie Clive smiled.

"You get your own bed," said Granny Cynthie, laughing merrily.

My eyes nearly burst out of my face.

Unless Granny and Grampie were going to sleep on the floor or in the en-suite bathroom — one in the shower and the other in the bath — then I couldn't see how this was going to work.

"No, it's okay, Granny and Gramps," I said, feeling

guilty that I was probably coming across as a bit bratty. "I don't mind sleeping on the floor."

"Ha! No need," said Grampie as he walked over to another door, that I had assumed was a wardrobe. He flung open the door — and stepped into another bedroom. "You'll have this bedroom all to yourself and we'll share the adjoining room with the twins."

At this point I was getting jaw ache; I just couldn't keep my mouth closed at everything I was seeing. This suite was **MASSIVE**, so massive that it had a whole other bedroom with its own bathroom attached to it.

Wow! Auntie Sharon really was a lottery millionaire to afford all of this.

My room had its own fridge, a massive TV — that almost took over a whole wall — and the balcony overlooked three of the hotel's pools. I thought I'd died and gone to swimming-pool heaven.

Sitting on my bed was like being on top of a white fluffy cloud, high in the sky. A swan-shaped towel floated happily next to me, for company. I did like my swan friend, but I wanted to speak to my real friends. I went to pull out my phone from my bag to send Arun, Charley and Evie a message about the hotel room, but then I decided not to, because I still hadn't heard from them.

Instead, I felt around my bag again, until I found it. I pulled out my treasure, the painted black, gold and green oval stone from my bag. Grandad's stone. I couldn't bring my globe or my wall map from home, but this was even better, I'd brought a part of Grandad to Jamaica with me. The cool stone warmed up in my hand. It felt like I had Grandad with me guiding me along the way.

THE FALLS

The next day, we were all up super-early because our bodies weren't used to being in a different country and time zone. It wasn't such a bad thing, because there was plenty we needed to fit into the day, including getting Dad to the wedding planner, so that he could show official papers like his passport and wedding certificate to make sure we could go ahead with the wedding vows' renewal ceremony.

Still, you can't really plan and do important things, like fooling your mother, on an empty stomach, can you? First things first, we enjoyed a delicious breakfast. My eyes filled with the sight of **FOOD GLORIOUS FOOD**, making me forget about the wedding planning for a long minute.

In the hotel's dining room, food stations overflowed with many international dishes: Asian, Italian, Mexican, American, Jamaican.

The Twinzies, Daz and I piled our plates high with stacks of waffles, pancakes with maple syrup, eggs "sunny side up" and crispy bacon.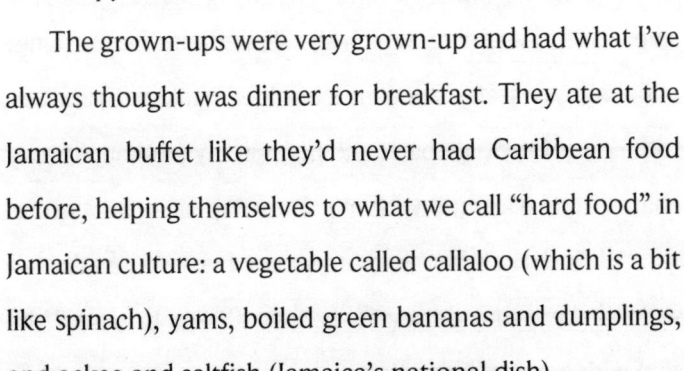

The grown-ups were very grown-up and had what I've always thought was dinner for breakfast. They ate at the Jamaican buffet like they'd never had Caribbean food before, helping themselves to what we call "hard food" in Jamaican culture: a vegetable called callaloo (which is a bit like spinach), yams, boiled green bananas and dumplings, and ackee and saltfish (Jamaica's national dish).

Dad, Granny and Grampie also had something called run down — a mackerel stew, made with vegetables and coconut milk, which they seemed to enjoy, but made me think I'd need the toilet if I ate it — but the big people, in particular, Dad, couldn't get enough of it.

There was even peppered steak on the menu – **FOR BREAKFAST!**

After breakfast, Dad delayed visiting the wedding planner, because Mum had booked for us to go to a place called Crystal Cove Falls. By the look of it, Mum had organized this holiday within an inch of our lives, with things to do every minute of the day.

Auntie Sharon told me to bring my notebook with me on the trip so that we could find time to discuss the next steps for the wedding, which she slipped into her designer handbag. As well as the notebook, I'd taken Grandad's stone out of my backpack and put it in my pocket. A lucky charm to take around with me on my Jamaican adventure.

"We'll shake off your mum somewhere at the falls. It's so loud there that not even she'll be able to hear us," she said with a conspiratorial wink.

Auntie Sharon was right. Every muscle and nerve in my body danced in excitement as I craned my neck upwards and watched the tumbling waterfall as it roared. I couldn't believe we'd now have the chance to climb it. An adventure up a watery mountain.

At first, Auntie Sharon had grumbled because she wasn't very impressed with the flat water shoes she was told she had to wear to climb. She was keen to go up in her high heels. "I haven't worn flats since I was seventeen," she protested, but the tour guide was having none of it. Auntie Sharon winced, and reluctantly put her shoes away in a locker, but insisted on keeping her designer handbag over her shoulder, as it had my notebook in it.

We made a human chain as we climbed, the cool water gushing past our feet as we made our way up and over steep grey stones.

Auntie Sharon was grateful for the flat shoes in the end. She, Dad, the Twinzies and I climbed the falls at a pace with the lead tour guide, while Dennis and Daz — who had both been let in on the secret about the wedding — were put in charge of delaying Mum's climb, so that the rest of us could plot our next steps. A little further on, we dipped underneath a small bridge that protected us from the splash of the gushing water. The water cascaded over the top of the bridge and around us. Auntie Sharon whipped my notebook out of her handbag and passed it to me. We were in a watery office, having a secret meeting under the sea.

"Right, Brains, what's first on your list?" asked Auntie Sharon.

Everyone looked at me expectantly.

"Well..." I started, slightly nervous with the weight of responsibility and knowing that Mum and the others would be hot on our heels. I tapped at the stone in my pocket and grew in confidence. "Dad needs to get his paperwork sorted when we get back from the falls, and then you and I need to meet with the wedding planner to talk about what we want the wedding to look like."

"Ooh yes, I have plenty of ideas," said Auntie Sharon, gleefully.

Dad gave me a look which I interpreted as, "Keep your aunt under control. PLEASE."

"After you get the boring paperwork bit done, Dad, you can start thinking about what you'd like to say to Mum on the big day. Somewhere as beautiful as these falls should help inspire you." I glanced over at Auntie Sharon, which reminded me of her and Dennis calling each other Shazzy

Bear and Mr Snuggles. "But try not to be too slushy or mushy," I told him.

"Oh, right," said Dad. "Not too slushy or mushy. How about something Shakespearean? 'A horse, a horse, my kingdom for a horse.'" Dad flung his arms around dramatically as he delivered the line.

The rest of us gave Dad side-eyed glances. Being so high up had clearly made him light-headed.

"Um, less horsey," I suggested.

"Yes, less horsey. How about 'Shall I compare thee to a summer's day?'"

That sounded better, but somehow familiar.

"Yep. Getting there, Dad. Keep working on it."

Dad nodded.

"Twinzies, you need to help keep Mum occupied. And don't forget the secret code."

The Twinzies patted the tops of their heads frantically. I gave them a double thumbs up. Perfect.

"No, we're patting because MUM'S COMING UP RIGHT BEHIND YOU," yelled Lena.

We turned to see Daz, Dennis and Mum dipping their

heads under the stony bridge. I passed Auntie Sharon the notebook behind my back, and she slipped it into her handbag. Fortunately, Mum hadn't heard Lena's bellow over the tumbling water.

"Ooh, is this a secret meeting. Can I join in?" asked Mum.

"NO, YOU CAN'T!" shouted Peter over the din of the waterfall.

Mum looked a bit put out.

"What we mean, Mum, is that there's no time to lose. We were waiting for you slowcoaches. Off we go!"

The Twinzies took one hand each and dashed off with Mum.

This water had two speed settings — fast and hard! It rushed past us in foamy white waves as we made our way further up the falls, clambering over the large stepping stones, as if we were walking up a staircase made by a giant. Pools of water, like mini swimming pools, carved and shaped out of the stone by the ebb and flow of the water, were too tempting not to get into. I stood in one of the little rock pools and let the water flow over my head, gasping as the surging ripples literally took my breath away. It was so much fun! I heard Mum's nagging cry as she protested for me not to get my hair wet, because I didn't have my swimming cap on. But then I saw a hint of a smile on her face and she let me carry on. Meanwhile, Dad was doing a lot of pausing and reflecting on his journey up the climb. He threw his arms out towards the green forests and flowing waters as if he was summoning inspiration from the views all around him.

"Wow, your dad is really connecting with his surroundings, so lovely to see him so... animated," said Mum. I nodded and smiled sweetly, making a note in my head that I needed to stop Dad from throwing his arms about so wildly before he started making Mum too suspicious, and also before he did himself or someone else an injury.

By the time we'd finished the climb, it felt like we were on top of the world. I was an explorer, not quite Woni Spotts, who has visited every country in the world, or Matthew Henson, the brilliant African-American Arctic explorer, but I was happy with my own adventure. I breathed in deeply, catching my breath, then patted the Jamaican stone in my shorts pocket. Maybe I could do new things and enjoy them. But could I also organize a secret second wedding? Well, that would prove to be another hill to climb.

POOL PARTY

Mum was hard to shake. A bit like set concrete. Until, that is, she had an accidental accident.

In the afternoon, after we'd got back from Crystal Cove Falls, Mum decided that we should all relax together at the beach. We persuaded her to go to the swimming pools instead, thinking it would be easier to lose her that way in the maze of six pools.

"Haven't you lot had enough of getting wet? I certainly have." Mum laughed but relented.

The Twinzies, Daz and I chose Splash World as the first pool we wanted to try. It has **FIVE** slides! And boy did we slide down every single one of them over and over again.

Mum didn't get in. We tried to encourage her to join Auntie Sharon and Dennis at the grown-ups only pool, but she insisted on staying with us and watching. Even though Dad was there.

"An extra pair of eyes is always a good thing. You can never be too careful where water's concerned," she said as she plonked herself down. Mum managed to sit bolt upright on the laid-back sun lounger, her eyes peeled like a hawk's, watching our every move.

To be honest, Mum was probably keeping a closer eye on Dad, because he was up and down those slides like a window cleaner on a ladder having "just one more go". The Twinzies held onto him tightly as they all flew down the slides shouting **"WHEEEEEEEEE"**, as if they were on the best fairground ride ever.

I stopped splashing and laughing for a moment and looked across at Mum. She'd now put her sunglasses and floppy sun hat on. But she hadn't even opened the book that she'd brought to help her relax.

There was no distracting Mum from her lifeguard duties and I was wary that Miss Babette, the wedding planner, could call on Dad at any point to come and see her in her office.

Auntie Sharon, like a secret code breaker in the war, was supposed to send word to us when Miss Babette was free. Auntie Sharon was still hanging out at the grown-ups only pool, where you could swim up to a bar and order any drink you liked. I just had to hope that Auntie Sharon didn't get too carried away with the free cocktails and then literally get carried away on an inflatable. I'd asked Dennis to keep an eye on her. Dennis is very sensible like that.

Other distractions began to creep in. Daz met a new "friend" in the pool that afternoon, a girl called Tiffany. She's from Texas. (I made a mental note to pop that in my Things and Places of Interest book later and to put a yellow dot on my world map when I got home.) Whilst Daz was showing off in front of Tiffany from Texas, jumping and splashing about like an excitable dolphin, I got out of the pool and went over to Mum.

"Mum, why don't you go and find Auntie Sharon in the grown-ups' pool? It's probably a bit noisy for you here. I bet Auntie Sharon wouldn't mind swapping with you and ~~spying on us~~ watching us for a bit, while you read your book and have a proper relax."

A spark seemed to alight in Mum; her face brightened.

I felt a bit guilty then. Really, I wanted to free Dad so that he could meet the wedding planner.

But Mum looked lovingly over at Dad. I think she wanted to spend time with him, but they were always so busy with us kids. Maybe wedding planning could wait, just for a little while?

"I tell you what, why don't you and Dad go to the pool, and I'll go with the Twinzies to the Kids' Club," I suggested. "Then you don't have to worry about us being on our own? Daz can stay here."

Mum and I looked over at Daz as he made a sound like Tarzan and did a cannonball running jump into the pool.

The most you can usually get out of my laid-back cousin is a bit of a mumble. This was a new Daz.

"Well, I suppose so," said Mum. "That's if you can get your dad out of Splash World. He looks to be having the time of his life. At least this holiday has got him away from his laptop and spreadsheets. Even though he's not remembered our upcoming anniversary...but DON'T tell him I said that."

"I won't," I sang happily, trying to throw Mum off the scent. But then she looked disappointed that I said I wouldn't tell. I just can't work out grown-ups, I wish they'd be clear about what they actually want.

Anyway, this wasn't the time for Mum to be wallowing about forgotten anniversaries. If only she knew what we had in store for her. I called the Twinzies and Dad out of the pool, patting my head three times so that the Twinzies would know that we were currently on a mission and wouldn't complain too much about leaving.

We walked over in the direction of the grown-up's pool. As we approached, Auntie Sharon, dressed in a bright pink bikini and matching pink sarong, dashed towards us.

"Are you leaving?" said Mum. "We were coming to join you once we settle Sunshine and the twins into Kids' Club."

Auntie Sharon looked as if she urgently needed to speak to Dad and me. She started patting at her head, then blinking and gesticulating in every direction.

"Why don't you go and grab those spare two sunloungers over there, Cheryl? I'll join you in a bit once I've dropped the kids off at the club," said Dad.

Mum hesitated but the Twinzies didn't think twice and pulled her off in the direction of the chairs.

"Nice work, Tone," said Auntie Sharon. "We needed to shake Cheryl quick time. We've had word from one of the pool attendants that Miss Babette has a tight window where she can see you in fifteen minutes. Tony, you need to get up to your room, get your legal papers and then get yourself over to her office sharpish. It's a shame because you're about to miss a great pool party. There's a DJ now and everything." Auntie Sharon looked back over to the pool longingly where it looked like the adults were getting ready to party.

I took my swimming cap off that Mum had insisted I put on to go in the pool; the sun was now burning down on me. I patted the top of my head rapidly to try and cool it down. I didn't realize what I was doing until it was too late.

I opened my mouth and shouted **"STOPPPPPPPPPPPPP!"** but it was no good, the DJ's music was too loud for the Twinzies to hear me. They had taken the secret head-patting code at its word, and knew they had to distract Mum quickly. Before Mum had a chance to take off her sunglasses, sun hat, kimono, or even her flip-flops, the Twinzies had swung into action and pushed her.

Mum flew like a diving bird into the swimming pool! But in a more inelegant bellyflop kind of way.

Dad, Auntie Sharon and I gasped and clung to each other in horror as Mum emerged from the water gasping, her maxi beach kimono with balloon sleeves billowing around her, like inflatable armbands. We were absolutely going to be deader than the oldest, deadest dodo.

The DJ stopped playing the music. Everyone stared at

the clothed woman spluttering in the water.

But then suddenly people around the pool started clapping and cheering. As the DJ cranked up the music again, loads of grown-ups started jumping into the pool around Mum. This had turned into a pool party with a twist!

"PAARTAAAY in the house!" someone shouted.

"Look at the way she even managed to keep her book from getting wet," shouted another pool-party person. It was true, Mum was holding her book out of the water like she was the Statue of Liberty.

"We have a new Queen of the Pool!" said the DJ from across the decks.

"What's your name, Hun?" a woman with a big smile asked Mum.

Then all of the people in the pool started chanting Mum's name. "Cheryl! Cheryl! Cheryl!" Mum seemed confused at first, as she stood in the water, holding her book in one hand and clinging to her sun hat with the other. But then she looked around at everyone cheering her name and beamed.

"I can't believe it. She's the new ME," cried Auntie Sharon in disbelief. She whistled through two of her fingers. "Way to go, Cheryl. Way to go! BIG UP YOURSELF!"

Dad didn't know what to do. Did he stay with Mum, tell the Twinzies off, or leave?

"Go! Go! Go!" said Auntie Sharon, with a wave of her hand. She then jumped into the pool, her sarong fanning like pink flamingo feathers behind her, while Dad made a dash for it.

"Is Mum all right?" asked Lena, her bottom lip quivering.

"We panic pushed!" said Peter.

"Well…yes, you certainly did. Don't worry, it was my fault, I accidentally patted my head… But, you know what? Mum seems to be absolutely…fine."

Mum climbed out of the pool with the grace of a goddess. Auntie Sharon started whooping and cheering

Mum's name again, and the swimming pool crowd went wild.

The Twinzies and I looked, opened-mouthed, at the scenes around us. I wished I'd had my phone to take pictures but then I hadn't looked at it again since I thought I'd been annoying my friends.

The DJ put an inflatable gold crown on Mum's head. She was now officially the Pool Party Queen. I'd never seen her look so shocked, but yet, strangely, so delighted. Even the Twinzies avoided a massive telling-off. Mum just said all the excitement of being on the pool slides and in the hot sun had "gone to their heads".

It was mission accomplished, in a completely unexpected way. Dad was off to officially seal the deal with the planner so the wedding could go ahead. Now we just had to put on the wedding of the year for Mum. She'd already been to the pool party of the year.

"That's enough excitement to last me a lifetime!" laughed Mum.

Little did Mum or we know what lay ahead.

MISS BABETTE

Miss Babette, the wedding planner, had been busy with other weddings, so she didn't have time to meet with Auntie Sharon and me until the day before we were supposed to leave the hotel to spend time with our family in Clarendon.

We enjoyed the rest of the week, playing beach football and volleyball, splashing in the crystal-clear ocean, zipping up and down the slides at Splash World, eating jerk sausages and jerk burgers at the Jerk Hut on the beach, as well as all the ice cream, cakes and fruit that we could manage at the buffets. The Twinzies weren't very pleased when they found out that the ice creams I'd promised to buy them were actually free, but they forgave me because we were having such a good time.

Mum kept trying to hint at Dad about their upcoming anniversary. *"Ooh, it feels so SPECIAL to be here in Jamaica, especially as we've never been here for any SPECIAL dates before..."* "It only feels like *FIFTEEN years since I was last here in Jamaica..."* But Dad was having none of it. He was devoted to the cause.

"Your mum's vexed," said Auntie Sharon, shaking her head. "We better get this surprise sorted quick, before she clobbers him over his noggin with the inflatable party crown she won at the swimming pool. We'll focus on the cake when we get to Clarendon. We'll hit the shops in town there. The effort will be worth it in the end."

I hoped so.

By the time Auntie Sharon and I walked into Miss Babette's office, we felt quietly confident about the wedding, even though our focus might have lapsed for a few days. Miss Babette soon burst our bubble.

Dressed in a dark grey suit and white blouse, Miss Babette looked very proper, but wore a daring dash of red lipstick, tying in with her long red fingernails with jewelled-studded tips, which added that extra bit of wedding sparkle. Auntie Sharon gave a radiant smile of approval.

"Well, Mizz Williams, this is a new experience for us, arranging a wedding in such a short amount of time. People usually spend months, years, planning such things — even for a renewal of vows ceremony. But we'll do our very best to create an experience that your guests will talk about for years to come."

Miss Babette's accent reminded me of how my Glammy Pepper speaks: a mix of Jamaican with a splash of American twang — Jamerican.

"Now, to the particulars, what kind of theme are you thinking of, my dears?"

Auntie Sharon took a deep breath and then reeled off a list of the "particulars" she was after. I hadn't discussed this in any detail with Auntie Sharon yet, and I was glad that she hadn't mentioned her "particulars" to Dad, because the second wedding would almost certainly have been well and truly called OFF. Dad valued his life far too much to have to face the wrath of Mum.

"Well, we'd like to hold it on the beach, and I was thinking along the lines of a fairground theme," Auntie Sharon began. "A few rides would be great. I know we couldn't do a rollercoaster, but could we hire some bumper cars or some spinning teacups for the kids? Trapeze artists, fire eaters and jugglers would go down nicely — and what about wild horses galloping across the beach? Not too many, perhaps three or four. We could do with a reggae artist too. We could fly in Maxi Priest. Cheryl and Tony both like him. Or someone more local like Sean Paul or Shaggy? Ooh, and did you ever see the 2012 London Olympic Games when the Queen jumped out of a plane just like James Bond? If we can get Tony to do something like that — and then have fireworks set off at the end of the day — now that would say SHA-BANG! It would be the ultimate romantic gesture, don't you think?"

Miss Babette's jaw dropped to the floor. "My dear, I

meant more the colours of the table dressings for the reception. We simply, not even in six months — EVER — could arrange all of that, let alone in less than two weeks. And as for the costs of something so elaborate—"

"No expense spared," cried Auntie Sharon, who I imagined was about to whip out a suitcase filled with cash, in sheer desperation.

"I'm sorry, Mizz Williams. NO. CAN. DO." There was no "my dear" about it this time.

"Oh," said Auntie Sharon, disappointment teeming in her voice. "I guess money can't buy everything."

The air in the room suddenly fell flat — all of our high hopes for Mum and Dad's second wedding sucked into a vacuum of stifling air.

I desperately wanted to rescue the situation. What colours did Mum like? Think, Sunshine, think. Brown, beige, cream — and that colour she liked to paint our walls in. Magenta? No, not magenta. Magnolia! Yes, that was the colour Mum was in love with — but on second thoughts, it wasn't very exciting at all.

"Um, I don't know if this will help," I started hesitantly,

"but my mum quite likes simple...classic things." I tried to be diplomatic, so that I didn't hurt Auntie Sharon's feelings. But her face was downcast. "And maybe a splash of orange or gold, to brighten things up a bit," I added, to try and make her feel better.

It was a tough balance. I knew if Auntie Sharon was allowed to get carried away, we would be getting fireworks, including a human one in the shape of Mum going off like a skyrocket. I'd also promised Dad I'd keep an eye on Auntie Sharon and rein in her wild ideas. But then, the wedding did need a bit of pizzazz to make it truly special.

Miss Babette's eyes sparkled as brightly as her nails. "Ah, if sophisticated elegance is what you're after, then you have knocked on the door of the right hotel, my dear. We guarantee that this will be a ceremony that no one will ever forget."

Enthusiasm sprang back into Auntie Sharon's face.

"And do you have a particular cake in mind?" asked Miss Babette.

Auntie Sharon nodded gleefully. "Oh yes, we plan to get something when we're in Clarendon. We'd like to arrange that ourselves. I've seen a great shop on the internet."

Miss Babette nodded. "Very well. And what about the dress, my dears? A bride's choice of dress often says a lot about how the day should be."

The dress? WHAT DRESS? I hadn't written that down in my notebook. There was me talking about how the cake was the most important thing about a wedding but what's more important on a bride's big day than her whopping, great dress?

Auntie Sharon's beaded plaits nearly stood on end.

We'd completely forgotten that Mum would need something to wear on the big day.

"My dears, the bride does have a wedding outfit, does she not?"

Auntie Sharon and I looked across at each other like naughty schoolchildren.

"We forgot," we confessed.

Miss Babette glanced at her watch for no other reason, I guessed, than to show we were wasting her time.

"My dears, you will need to confirm the menu and

your guest list, so that we can cook your loved ones the meal of their dreams. We will also take care of decorations and entertainments. But time is of the essence, there's only ten days until the wedding. You arrange the cake and the dress, and we can do the rest."

And that was that. Miss Babette swept us out of the room in a flash. Now added to our Things to Do List was finding one of the fussiest people in the universe — my mum — a suitable wedding outfit, without her knowing. Getting Dad to jump out of a plane would be an easier task.

"Maybe we could fly in your mum's old wedding dress from England?" cried Auntie Sharon.

I had a sudden vision of our elderly neighbour, Mrs Turner, scrambling up a ladder to retrieve Mum's wedding dress from a suitcase in our dusty attic.

"Um, I think we might need to think of other alternatives, Auntie Sharon," I replied, bursting her bubble of hope.

"Ack, it's fine. We'll just shop for a cake and a dress when we get to Clarendon. If there's one thing I can do it's

S.H.O.P. Shop till I drop!" Auntie Sharon fist-pumped the air.

But Mum had been so insistent about us doing everything together as a family when we got to Clarendon, including going up to Grandad Bobby's family home, Old Farm, to meet my Great-Aunt Vi and her family. When would we find the time to shop for a wedding dress and a cake without her in tow?

I thought about how long it had taken me to organize my suitcase for the holiday — and how in the end I needed Mum's help to do it. How were we going to get all of this done? I touched the stone in my pocket for a bit of comfort. We'd have to find a way.

We put off telling Dad about the wedding dress drama until the next day, when we were about to leave for Clarendon. Mum was at the reception desk talking about our return to the hotel for the third week of our holiday. I'd asked Daz to keep an eye on her, but he was too busy whispering sweet nothings into Tiffany from Texas's ear

(UGH!). Daz must be really funny because Tiffany kept giggling every three seconds and saying things like *"Daz, y'all so funny"*, and repeatedly tossing her long braids back and forth over her shoulder — until they ended up flying into Daz's eyes. I know I'm about to be a teenager in the not-too-faraway future, but teenagers can sometimes be very...odd.

The Twinzies and Grampie and Granny were outside waiting for the taxi, so we seized our chance to grab Dad. He threw one hand up to his bald head in dismay. "How are we going to find Cheryl a dress in time for the wedding in TEN DAYS' TIME? It takes her a month to decide when buying a jumper," said Dad, speaking out loud what I had been running over in my head since the meeting with Miss Babette. Dad had spoken a bit louder than he'd meant to, which immediately attracted Mum's attention. She hurried over to us. (Daz was still dealing with his watering eyes from Tiffany's hair lashing, so couldn't stop her.)

"What's happened? What about ten days' time?" said Mum urgently.

We all clammed up, unable to find words to explain

ourselves out of the situation quickly enough. I started patting my head in desperation for the Twinzies to run in and rescue us. (Without them pushing Mum into a nearby plant pot — hopefully.)

"Sunshine, what's wrong with your head?" demanded Mum.

Auntie Sharon joined in. She patted her head and started rubbing her tummy. "Ooh, yes, let's have a game of trying to pat your head and rubbing your tummy at the same time, it's almost impossible, isn't it?"

"Yes, it is," agreed Dad, joining in.

Mum looked at us as if she needed to cart us all off for a long lie-down.

It was no use, the Twinzies hadn't seen us — and we were starting to draw attention from passers-by. We'd been **BUSTED**.

"Okay, maybe the game's up—" started Dad.

But...

NO WAY!

What I can only describe as a walking miracle happened next.

Something across the lobby area caught Auntie Sharon's eye. "It can't be," she mouthed, removing her sunglasses from her face as if to confirm with her own two eyes what – or should I say whom – she thought she was seeing. Auntie Sharon grabbed Mum's hand and pulled her in the direction of the lifts.

"Sharon, what on earth has possessed you? We're supposed to be leaving the hotel not going back up to our rooms. And why were you all rubbing your tummies and patting your hea—"

When Mum clapped her eyes on who Auntie Sharon had been looking at, she completely forgot about what she'd been saying.

A tall man with movie star looks was standing near the lifts. As it turns out, it *was* a movie star, and even more special, it was one of Mum's most favourite-ever actors.

"Excuse me, I hope you don't mind us bothering you, Mr Idris Elba, but my sister here is such a big fan of yours," sang Auntie Sharon.

Mum looked terrified – as if Mr Elba had just shouted "boo" at her and wasn't someone she swooned over every time she saw him on telly.

"Would you mind if we took a picture with you?" asked Auntie Sharon.

Mum was speechless.

Mr Elba stepped forward and smiled a movie star glowing smile for the camera. Mum, her body rigid with shock at seeing the actor of her dreams, adjusted her facial expression from outright fright to a frozen grin.

The movie star beamed at Mum, which made her legs go all quivery, as if the earth had moved under her feet. She still couldn't speak but managed to ring out a high-pitched squeal of excitement like a squeaky duck, that sounded a bit like this "SQUEEEEEAAAAP".

"Sunshine, why don't you escort your mum to the taxi?" Auntie Sharon winked at me. I didn't know what the wink meant but took the hint to skedaddle with Mum and leave Auntie Sharon to it. Though it was quite difficult to move her. Dad and I had to cajole Mum, like a couple of sheepdogs rounding-up a stray sheep, out of the front doors and into the waiting taxi to join the rest of our family.

I breathed a sigh of relief. The secret mission was still intact. Fancy seeing Mum's favourite actor. That was a turn up for the books. Who would show up next? I almost expected to turn round and find The Rock or Zendaya behind me. I took a sneaky look, just in case. Nah, they weren't there.

I touched the stone in my pocket. Grandad would have loved this moment, but even he'd say that was a near miss too close for comfort. Thank goodness for the distracting power of celebrities.

15

CLARENDON

Mum stared out of the window dreamily and fanned herself with her flip-out fan throughout the entire hour and a half drive to Clarendon, even though there was air con in the taxi.

The good news was that she had completely forgotten to grill Auntie Sharon, Dad and me about what we were talking about in the hotel lobby, and why we were rubbing our tummies and patting our heads. The unwelcome news was, we now had a wedding dress as well as a cake to sort out — and the clock was ticking.

I needed a distraction. **MY PHONE!** I hadn't switched it on to send my friends any more pictures or messages for days. I hadn't wanted them to think I was up my own bottom showing off about all the luxuries of the holiday.

I pulled the phone out of my rucksack and switched it on, looking out of one eye when it sprang into life.

MESSAGES.

Lots of them. Like these:

"Are you okay, Sunny?"

"HEY! Where are you?????"

"Sunny, we are REALLY worried!!!!!"

"???????!!!!!!!!!"

I threw my hand to my mouth. The last time I'd messaged my friends was when I'd sent them a selfie of me with the sandy beach and sea behind me and foolishly — and selfishly — hadn't thought that they might actually have replied and been worried after seeing no response from me.

I scrolled back through the messages to see photos that they had sent me from DAYS ago.

Charley had sent me a selfie of her standing in the middle of somewhere grassy and green with craggy cliffs towering in the distance behind her. It must have been a windy day because her red bob was swept across her face, but you could still see her huge smile as she did a thumb's up for the photo.

Evie's selfie was of her on a ship's deck with open sea behind her. She had winked for the camera.

Arun's was standing in front of a big white house with three of his little cousins crowding around him. Arun had his sunglasses on. Being cool.

"Hello from Ireland!" said Charley's message.

"Greetings from India!" said Arun's.

"Hello from the sea!" said Evie's, mysteriously.

I grinned. My friends didn't think I was showing off at all and looked like they were having a great time themselves.

I quickly typed a group message.

"HELLO, from the open road! I'm on my way to see my family in Clarendon. I am SO sorry I haven't been in touch. You look like you're all having a great time, I'm so glad! I promise I'll message from now on!"

I held my phone in my hand waiting for their reply. With us taking photos and being able to send messages to each other, my friends didn't feel so far away, after all.

Looking out of the window, on the road to Clarendon, open land stretched out as far as the eye could see, while towering hills dotted with scattered houses dominated the view in the distance. The hazy sun stayed hidden, for now, behind them. The heat seemed to thicken as we moved further away from the sea and hit Clarendon, as if we were cooking in a Jamaican Dutch pot. I had a quick look in my notebook to check out facts I had looked up at home to distract myself from the heat.

Clarendon is a parish in the county of Middlesex. Jamaica has three counties: Cornwall, Surrey and Middlesex, and they link back to Jamaica's ties with Britain. My grandparents always told me how they had to study about Britain when they were in school in Jamaica. Granny Cynthie said that when she was a little girl, she dreamed that one day she would end up going to Buckingham Palace and having tea with the Queen, but she never did!

Eventually, we turned onto a dusty, tree-lined drive which offered welcome shade from the heat. We pulled up in front of my Great-Aunt Joy's sunshine yellow house, which sat all on its own, at the end of the canopy of trees.

Like many of the homes I'd seen on my journey through Jamaica, it was on one level. A covered veranda swept from one side of the house to the other.

As we got out of the minibus taxi, a familiar face came out of the front door to greet us, dressed in a cool, white linen dress.

Glammy Pepper flung open her arms from the veranda, as if it was her stage and she was greeting her audience. "Family, welcome home," she sang.

"Glammy!" shouted the Twinzies, as they ran up the three steps of the veranda and into Glammy's arms, almost sending her toppling over. Glammy cackled that loud laugh of hers, which reminds me of a mash-up between a whistling kettle and a dolphin.

"Sunshine and Daz, you too big to give your glam-ma a kiss," shouted Glammy. Even Daz smiled then. He'd been sulking since we left the hotel after being separated from his beloved *"she's not my girlfriend, we're just good friends"* Tiffany from Texas.

Glammy held us all tightly and I disappeared into the hazy mist of her honeysuckle-scented perfume.

Once we'd piled all our bags out of the minibus, Glammy Pepper gestured to some seats on the veranda.

"Come sit, you've had a long journey, tell me all about how you've spent your first week in paradise. Joy has made some fresh lemonade and should be out any minute."

Right on cue, my Great-Aunt Joy shuffled backwards out of the front door. She turned to face us, revealing a tray complete with a jug of lemonade and glasses. I almost did a double take. In one way, she was the complete mirror image of Glammy Pepper — her face was the same, bright eyes, pursed lips, long nose and high cheekbones — but her clothing was completely different from my glamorous grandmother. She wore a plain cream T-shirt and a pleated beige skirt — and her hair was completely grey and in two long plaits, like a style Mum does for me to keep my hair "neat and functional".

Dad took the tray from Great-Aunt Joy. She thanked

him with a shy smile and then wiped at her brow with the back of her hand. She seemed the same, yet completely different from Glammy Pepper in her manner, too.

"Twinzies, this is *my* twinzie. My sister. Your Great-Aunt Joy," said Glammy, with a smile.

Twins ran in our family.

The Twinzies gawped at Great-Aunt Joy as if she'd just popped in for a visit from outer space. Seeing her in real life was different to seeing her on a picture or saying the occasional hello on the phone at Christmas and Easter.

"I knew you were twins, but you're identical!" gasped Lena.

Glammy and Great-Aunt Joy nodded happily.

"It's like all of us are quadruple twins," said Peter. "IMPRESSIVE."

Peter got up from his seat and hi-fived Lena, Glammy and Great-Aunt Joy.

Both sets of twins erupted into howls of laughter. It must be a twin thing.

"Howdeedo?" said Great-Aunt Joy, smiling widely. "Howdeedo!"

Everyone spoke at once then, telling Glammy and Great-Aunt Joy about the hotel and its swimming pools and food from around the world, and our trip to Crystal Cove Falls. Glammy and Great-Aunt Joy both cooed and said "ahh" at all our tales.

"And Daz has got a girl 'friend'," said Peter, wrapping his fingers around the word friend.

"She's Tiffany from Texas. In America," added Lena.

Daz looked up from his phone in fright. "She's not my girlfriend," he grunted.

"Yes, we know, you keep telling us that," said Peter, rolling his eyes. "But I've never seen you hold hands with any of your other friends before."

Daz buried his head back in his phone, while the rest of us stifled our giggles.

Fortunately for Daz, his blushes were spared by a new arrival.

16

ZIGGY

"Ah, here he comes," said Glammy, holding one hand up to shield her eyes from the shimmering sun and looking towards the end of the long drive.

I glanced over in the direction of where Glammy was looking.

Sure enough, a tall figure came into view. The shadow of the person, cast in a long arch by the sun, doubled their tall frame along the dusty ground.

The person walked towards us with shoulders sloped backwards. They seemed confident, but casual, like they hadn't a care in the world. As the person drew closer, I saw it was a boy of around my age. Maybe a little older. My cousin Ziggy! He looked very different from the dribbling toddler I'd seen in the old photo before we'd left for Jamaica.

"Ziggy, what time you call, this?" yelled Great-Aunt Joy, suddenly sounding as loud as Glammy Pepper always is.

"Sorry, Grandma, I was feeding Brian," replied Ziggy.

"You and that goat! I'm surprised you don't move him into your mother's house," teased Glammy Pepper.

"A goat? Can I meet him?" asked Peter, his face lighting up, but then he frowned. "We're not going to eat him for dinner, are we?"

For the first time, Ziggy lost his leisurely swagger. He suddenly looked panicked. "NO!" he shouted.

Glammy Pepper and Great-Aunt Joy giggled as if they were secretly in on a great joke. "We're not going to eat Brian," tittered Great-Aunt Joy. "He's Ziggy's best friend!"

"Though he might be nice seasoned up with a few peppers and onions, and served with rice and dumplings," cried Glammy Pepper.

Glammy and Great-Aunt Joy roared with laughter, and

that's when I saw how easy they were in each other's company, bouncing off each other's one-liners and as mischievous as the Twinzies when they're cooking up trouble together.

Ziggy still looked horrified.

"Hush, Ziggy, we're just teasing. Brian is completely safe." Great-Aunt Joy smiled warmly.

"Oh, you got my T-shirt," Granny Cynthie said to Ziggy, moving the subject away from goat dinners. He was wearing a football shirt that Granny had sent him as a gift before we left for Jamaica.

A month before the trip, Granny had sent a barrel packed with everything from clothes to a first-aid kit, school supplies — including a dictionary — to toiletries, and towels to tinned foods, like baked beans, jars of peanut butter and jam, and even clothes pegs. She'd explained to me why she was doing this after I'd seen the huge barrel-shaped container in the middle of her living room when I'd gone over to visit.

"It's tradition to send over a barrel with gifts to Jamaica," she'd said. "It isn't strictly necessary now, not like in the old days when you'd send over things that your loved ones couldn't easily buy, but in this modern newfangled world with its googly internet and microwave phones, I want to hold onto something that I find dear. Some of these things are still expensive in Jamaica and some things will come in handy for us when we're over there."

My cousin Lorna, Ziggy's mum, had "received" the barrel once it had arrived in Jamaica. Then she'd handed out the contents to all the people who were supposed to get them. That's how Ziggy had got his new football shirt.

"I might have to disown you if you keep wearing that Manchester United shirt," laughed Dad. "Unless I can persuade you to turn to the bright side, and support Aston Villa." Dad double shuffled his eyebrows.

Ziggy smiled, his fears for Brian ending up in a cooking pot eased.

"Come, Ziggy, have a glass of the best homemade lemonade I've ever tasted," called Grampie Clive. Not even Granny Cynthie, who is the best cook in the world EVER, could deny it.

Once we'd finished the lemonade, we brought our bags inside, freshened up and chatted some more, before settling down for an afternoon tea of curried patties wrapped in coco bread. After the meal, Ziggy stretched his long legs out from the sofa ready to spend the rest of the afternoon in relaxation. I think long legs run in my family.

"Uh-uh. You think your cousins reach all the way long from England to watch you sit on your behind?" called Great-Aunt Joy.

"Huh?" said Ziggy, half-sleepy from the delicious afternoon tea. He yawned. "Okay, Grandma. We can play some games on the PlayStation. I've brought it with me in my backpack."

Great-Aunt Joy's eyes nearly flew out of their sockets. "Bwoy, what's wrong with you? I said get up off your behind. Your cousins didn't travel all this way to do something they can play at home. Show them authentic Jamaica. Play with them properly — and give them a taste of the island."

"Authentic Jamaica?" questioned Ziggy. I got the feeling that Ziggy didn't want to spend most of his own summer holidays showing his English cousins "authentic Jamaica". His face looked like he'd been slapped with a wet fish.

Great-Aunt Joy gave him a stare so hard that even Paddington Bear would have said "respect".

"Right! Authentic Jamaica, it is!" Ziggy jumped to his feet. "Let's go!"

"Go where?" asked the Twinzies excitedly.

"For a taste of authentic Jamaica, of course. You ready?"

Daz stayed put on the sofa glued to his phone, messaging Tiffany from Texas back at the hotel, no doubt. Ziggy marched the Twinzies and me out into the front garden and stopped.

"The tourists need a tour," he said, bowing at me in a very sarcastic way. I'm not sure he was taking his tour guide duties very seriously. "If we're lucky, we might be able to fit in a few games on the station later, hey, Likkle Pete and Lee-Lee?" Ziggy winked at the Twinzies.

Ziggy's personality was certainly living up to the photo I'd seen of him as a cheeky-faced toddler. But by the look of it he seemed to prefer the Twinzies to me, even though we were closer in age. He was already giving them nicknames! I suddenly felt awkward, as if I didn't belong. If my own cousin didn't like me, what chance did I have at a new school with a load of strangers?

"What happened to you? You see a ghost?" said Ziggy. "Hey, Cuz, is there anyone in there?"

Ziggy was talking to me, waving his hands in front of my face to wake me out of my faraway thoughts. I realized my mouth was half-open. Instead of speaking, I just shuffled awkwardly and said nothing. Ziggy tilted his head, raised questioning eyebrows at me, and smiled. Great! Now he'd think I was a sulky, strange boring fool. If I could have clicked my heels three times to send myself home, or better still, down a deep, dark well to hide from the shame of being awkward me, I would have done. Oof! Why am I always so much like me?

"Come on, daydreamer," he said, smiling broadly at me now. "Let's have another feast." Ziggy extended his arm and gestured around the garden inviting the Twinzies and me to see what he meant.

Red and orange ripe mangoes glistened on their branches. This garden was full of fruit trees.

"They're mangoes," said Ziggy, seeing me look up at them. I don't think he was trying to be funny. He genuinely thought I'd never seen a mango before.

I gave him a look. "We do eat mangoes in England," I said, laughing now. "From the shops, though — not from trees like this."

Ziggy grinned. "Ha! But what kind of mango are they?" He thought he had me then.

My mind traced back to all the types of mangoes that Grandad Bobby had told me about. And it made me smile to think of him and his sister, my Great-Aunt Vi, climbing their mango tree at Old Farm, where we'd be going in a few days' time.

I tapped a finger against my lip. "Well, they could be Julie mangoes or East Indian mangoes. I don't think they're hairy mangoes. I'll take a guess at a Number 11 mango!"

Ziggy's jaw hit the ground. "Well look here at the mango queen."

He was in full stride now, warming to the occasion and

our knowledge of his home. He reached up and pulled four mangoes from one of the low hanging branches.

"Here, taste. Each type of mango has a different flavour, shape and texture. And a Number 11 is one of the best mangoes you'll ever taste anywhere in the world."

We peeled the skin back with our teeth and bit into the mango's orange, sweet flesh.

"Yum!" said Peter, licking the sticky juice from his fingers.

"It's the sweetest mango I've ever eaten," said Lena, excitedly.

It was — the Jamaican sunshine making it taste all the sweeter. Grandad's face used to light up when he would eat food from "back home", as if eating mango or

sugar cane or yams or sweet potatoes were a special key to opening locked-away memories. I now could see why.

Next, Ziggy showed us something I'd never eaten before. He scooped a small, green, round fruit off another type of tree. They were growing in bunches, like grapes. He passed one each to us.

"These are guineps," said Ziggy. "My favourite fruit to eat all day long." Playing to his eager crowd, Ziggy bit into the skin of the fruit and pulled it apart to reveal a golf ball shaped, light-orange fruit inside the shell.

"It looks a bit like a lychee," said Peter. "I like those."

"Yes, eat the flesh and then spit out the seed," said Ziggy.

The Twinzies gladly gobbled down the jelly-like, sweet, yet sharp, fruit and spat out the seed as Ziggy had told them.

The Twinzies smiled as Ziggy picked two more bunches — and then a third.

We all ended up eating a bunch of the delicious guineps to ourselves, and then sat like a group of humpty dumpties, underneath the leafy guinep tree, leaning back against the trunk chatting like old friends.

"Hey, can we take a load of mangoes and guineps for

Mum and Dad's secret wedding?" asked Peter with a cheeky grin. And then he realized his mistake. He flung his hand to his mouth. "Oops, sorry, Sunny!"

Lena waved her fingers in front of Ziggy's eyes. "When I count to three, you'll forget what you've just heard. There is absolutely NO secret wedding being secretly organized for Mum and Dad next week at the Grand Beach Hotel, in Marine Bay."

I mean Lena might as well have given Ziggy the postcode for the hotel as well. Talk about going into the finer details. I rolled my eyes — kids!

Ziggy was cracking up laughing at us, but also had a look of confusion on his face. "Okay, okay, the wedding is forgotten. Though I thought your parents were already married?"

Ziggy seemed like an okay kind of person. After my first worries and doubts about getting on with him, I was beginning to think he'd make a nice friend, so I thought we might as well tell him. A burden shared is a burden solved, or some old saying like that. And he might be able to help us, though I wasn't sure how yet.

We told him about the wedding vows' renewal ceremony, because Mum and Dad would be celebrating their fifteen-year crystal wedding anniversary, and about how we needed a cake and a wedding dress by next week — and we were running out of time.

He nodded thoughtfully. "You know, my best friend is a great chef. That's what he wants to be when we graduate from school. How about you come over to my place tomorrow and I'll get him to come too and bake a cake? What about an authentic Jamaican fruit cake? And you can experience my authentic Jamaican kitchen." Ziggy smiled widely. "Likkle Pete and Lee-Lee, we can see if my chickens have laid any eggs. Let's make it a family affair!"

The Twinzies' eyes lit up.

"Okay," I said. "Why not! It'll be one less thing for Auntie Sharon to think about if we don't have to buy the cake in town."

We all lay back against the tree trunk, the fruit-laden branches sheltering us from the afternoon sun. This felt right. Me and my siblings and my cousin sitting together. It felt like home.

The afternoon seemed to fly by quite quickly after that.

Ziggy's Mum, Lorna, came by after work. Even in her high heels, she managed to run up onto the steps of the veranda to Mum and Auntie Sharon. They all jumped around in a circle like they were kids again.

"Oh, my dear cousins, I am the happiest person in the world to see you," said Lorna.

"Yes, it's been too long," said Mum, her eyes glistening with emotion.

"I've missed out on so much since your wedding, so much..." Lorna cut off then and embraced Mum and Auntie Sharon again tightly. They didn't have to say any more.

With the brightest of smiles she then hugged Daz, the Twinzies and me. "Look at these kids. So nice to see you and be able to give you a squeeze. And look how tall you all are!"

Peter went up onto his tiptoes to make himself seem even taller.

"You kids should have seen the trouble we used to cause my mum and your grandma when we were your age," said Lorna, with a chuckle.

"Don't tell them!" cackled Auntie Sharon. "You'll only start giving them ideas. And we have enough on our plate." She winked at me.

"And do you remember the games we used to play?" said Lorna. "Oh, Ziggy, you must show the kids some Jamaican games. Give them a taste of yard – old school style."

Ziggy smiled warmly and nodded. "How about tomorrow? They can come over to our place – and I'll introduce the twins and Sunshine to Brian." Ziggy was thinking on his feet. He had the perfect excuse for us to go over to his place for the cake-baking without Mum suspecting a thing.

Everyone agreed that would be a great idea.

As night fell, after a dinner of saltfish, cabbage, boiled green bananas and dumplings, my family sat on the veranda and looked up at the sea of stars. There were so many, like glistening diamonds lighting up the dark. They felt so close, as if I could reach up and pluck one straight from the sky and put it in my pocket. A shining star next to Grandad's earthy stone.

"Beautiful, isn't it?" said Dad, looking up at the night sky with me.

I smiled. "Everywhere we go, it's like we're in a living, breathing painting."

"Yes," said Lorna, joining in. "And with you all here, the painting is finally complete." She reached out and held Mum's and Auntie Sharon's hands tightly.

Mum teared up again.

Auntie Sharon broke through the serenity. She started slapping at her arms as if to slay an invisible beast.

"I think the mosquitoes are in love with you," chuckled Great-Aunt Joy.

"They're about to get down on one knee and propose," howled Glammy Pepper.

Dad, Auntie Sharon and I laughed nervously. The mention of marriage proposals was too close to home. Mum gave us a strange look.

But then we all settled down into more chat before it was time for bed.

Lorna offered to take the Twinzies, Daz and me for a sleepover, but Mum said she thought it best we all stay together, especially as Lorna would have to leave early in the morning for work. Honestly, can my mum ever let go? Anyway, Lorna and Ziggy said their goodbyes and he promised to walk back in the morning to take us over to his place.

The Twinzies, Daz and I slept in the living room on the sofa and a mattress on the floor, while the grown-ups had the beds with the protective mosquito nets.

"The older the juice, the sweeter the wine," said Auntie Sharon, swatting at her arm again. "You kids with your young blood will be fine. It's the vintage blood these pesky mozzies are after." Auntie Sharon nearly knocked herself out with a blow to her head as she swore she could feel one biting at her scalp.

I shuddered.

"Just watch out for the lizards. I'll never forget the day when I woke up in this very house when I was thirteen years old and saw a lizard on the wall behind me. I thought it was a wall ornament at first, until I saw it skedaddle across the wall and out of the window. I nearly jumped out of my skin and out of the window with it." Auntie Sharon cackled. "Night, night. Don't let the bedbugs bite."

Was that supposed to be a comforting bedtime story? Still, the animal tales didn't seem to affect the Twinzies, who were tucked in next to Brown Bunny and Betty the Bat, or Daz. They were asleep in no time, but I just couldn't rest.

I looked at my phone. My friends had sent more messages.

Charley: "O.M.G! We were so worried. Glad you're all right! GOOD LUCK with the wedding planning!"

Arun: "You scared us! REMEMBER, this wedding is going to be better than a Hollywood movie!"

Evie: "NEVER go missing for so long again, unless you

tell us you're going missing! YOU can do it! You've got this!"

"SORRY — and thanks!" I wrote back.

I hoped my friends would be my friends always and for ever even when we parted ways at high school.

I pulled my sheet up over my head, after tucking it tightly underneath my feet, to hide myself from any mosquitoes that might try to nip at my toes and the rest of my body, even though I was stifling with the heat. I must have resembled a mummy wrapped up in bandages, but I couldn't help it.

Crickets were singing to each other outside. They were party animals! I wished they'd keep the noise down. And then I could swear I saw shadows of lizards and all sorts of deadly creatures climbing across the walls and furniture. In between the animal spotting, my thoughts flitted around as if there was an eclipse of moths that had broken in and were jumping around my head.

It had been a good day. After only seeing pictures of them in photo albums, and hearing snatches of their voices on the phone on special occasions, we had finally met

Great-Aunt Joy and my cousins Ziggy and Lorna for real — and it was wonderful to catch up with Glammy Pepper again. Despite my first fears about Ziggy and me not getting along, I liked him very much. Maybe now we really would plan the wedding of the twenty-first century.

17

BRIAN THE GOAT AND "THE OTHERS"

"Never work with children or animals" is a phrase that grown-ups use sometimes. I found out they are right. Well, about the animals at least.

By the time the sun rose, streaming through the living room window, I was sure I hadn't had a wink of sleep all night. Though Auntie Sharon was right about mosquitoes not liking young blood, because I couldn't feel any itchy, stinging bites on me — which was a bonus.

I followed the delicious smells of fried plantain and cocoa tea, made with natural cocoa, cinnamon and condensed milk, wafting from Great-Aunt Joy's kitchen. The tea was as delicious as it smelled: hot, spicy, sweet and comforting.

As promised, Ziggy turned up for us early. Deliberately.

Mum wasn't even ready. She was still in her dressing gown and headscarf. "If you hang on, we'll all come with you," she said.

"Oh, don't worry, Cuz Cheryl," said Ziggy sweetly. "Mamma has left for work now anyway. But Miss Winnie, our housekeeper, will be there by the time I get back. I'll take these guys with me for the day and leave you big people to do whatever you big people do. You can come over later when Mamma's home. Have a nice relaxing day. I'll introduce the twins to Brian, like I said. You'd like that, wouldn't you, Likkle Pete and Lee-Lee?"

The Twinzies started jumping up and down and clapping their hands like overexcited seals waiting for a fishy breakfast. Ziggy made pleading moon eyes at Mum. She smiled at him. "Oh, you are so good. Thank you, Ziggy."

This boy was slick.

Daz was still fast asleep. He could sleep lying down in the middle of a noisy building site. We had no time to lose, so we left him to his gentle snoring.

It felt a bit unnerving leaving the comfort of Great-Aunt Joy's sunshine-yellow house and tree-lined garden as we hit the busy road. I didn't know where I was going, and this felt strange and new.

But the people we walked past were all so friendly. They said good morning and smiled at the Twinzies and me like they'd known us all our lives — and they told Ziggy to pass on their regards to his mother and grandmother. They reminded me of the way I would say hi to Mr Chanda, Mrs Flowers and Jakub the shopkeepers back at home. Grandad Bobby used to do it — so I've continued the tradition — and it made me wonder whether Grandad had continued this friendly tradition from what he had done in Jamaica.

"Is Brian the goat definitely home?" asked Peter, keenly, as if Brian could come and go as he pleased.

Ziggy laughed. "The last time I checked — YES. Unless he's made a run for it. He's a clever old goat. He's been known to escape out of his pen and get himself into all kinds of mischief. One time he ate Mum's panties. He jumped up and pulled them off the washing line. And all he did was stare at me with a haughty expression when I grabbed them out of his mouth, as if he was telling me they needed a bit of salt and pepper for extra seasoning. He's a facety old goat, but he's *my* old goat and I wouldn't have him any other way. And just wait till you meet the others."

I assumed by "the others" that Ziggy had meant the chickens who we were going to get the eggs from to make the wedding cake. Turns out I was wrong.

After a few more minutes of walking along, Ziggy swooped left and opened a gate. The Twinzies and I followed him, walking into a large garden — or yard as Jamaicans call it. Ziggy's house looked a little smaller than Great-Aunt Joy's; it was on one level again, with steps leading up to a veranda, and painted bright white.

A tall, brown, skinny dog came running towards us, jumping up onto Ziggy and then sniffing round our legs.

"Calm down, boy," said Ziggy, patting the dog on the head. "Don't mind Rudie. He just likes to get into everyone's business — that's why we call him Rudie. Always sticking his nose where it doesn't belong."

Peter and Lena let Rudie bury his snout into their hands, and around their pockets, as if he was trying to sniff out a treat.

"I LOVE dogs," said Lena.

"Wait until you meet Big Dog and Lion," said Ziggy.

Something about having animals called Big Dog and Lion made me a little nervous. My eyes darted around. Would two giant beasts launch themselves at me?

As we approached the front of the house, we saw a woman carrying a basket of washing out. I realized it must be Miss Winnie. She helped out while Lorna was at work, like a housekeeper.

"Hello, children," said Miss Winnie, with a wide smile. "So nice to meet you all. I know you want to bake — and I'm letting you do it on your own because it's a very nice gesture. But DON'T mess up the house."

Ziggy nodded his head, and turned on the charm with his radiant smile, which seemed to make grown-ups melt like butter in the hot sun.

"We won't," he said sweetly.

Miss Winnie chuckled heartily and went off into the garden.

Ziggy opened the front door of his house and two more dogs burst out of it as if they'd been waiting to escape for hours.

"This is Big Dog," said Ziggy, pointing to a small, black and white dog. We call him Big Dog because he's so small but throws himself around like he's a wolfhound."

Another dog, even smaller than Big Dog, golden brown, with a brown bushy tail and mane of golden-brown hair, yapped very 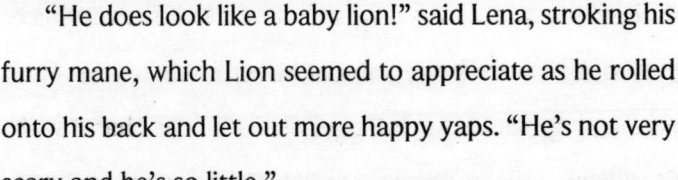 loudly for attention. "And this is Lion."

"He does look like a baby lion!" said Lena, stroking his furry mane, which Lion seemed to appreciate as he rolled onto his back and let out more happy yaps. "He's not very scary and he's so little."

"Wha'?! Don't let him hear you say that! He thinks

he's big and bad with that bark of his. But he has the heart of a lion, don't you, boy?"

Lion yapped a proud "yes". I felt myself laughing freely. All this newness was fun. And Ziggy was really cool.

"Come meet Brian!"

Ziggy introduced us to Brian in his pen. He patted the goat on the head, between his horns. "Hey, boy, these are my English cousins," said Ziggy softly.

Brian let out a long, deep bleat to greet us, which made us all burst into giggles. It was as if Brian could understand Ziggy.

"He needs company," said Ziggy, furrowing his eyebrows. "Goats should at least live in pairs, so I've convinced my parents to get Brian a playmate when my pops comes back from America."

Ziggy's dad works over in the US as a construction worker.

Brian let out a long, heartfelt bleat, as if in one hundred per cent agreement with Ziggy.

"Ziggy, are you Doctor Dolittle?" asked Peter in wide-eyed wonder.

"Hey, maybe I am," boasted Ziggy. "Here, watch this. Rudie, come give me a touch."

Rudie happily took part in the show. He stopped sniffing round the Twinzies' feet and padded over to Ziggy. Rudie lifted his paw and Ziggy gave him a fist bump.

"Good dog," said Ziggy, slipping a treat out of his pocket and feeding Rudie.

Sold! I have never wanted a pet as much as the Twinzies have, but I was beginning to get as excited as them. Would anyone notice if I smuggled Rudie, Big Dog and Lion back home on the plane with me? I could imagine Big Dog and Lion sitting in my seat happily yapping and Rudie roaming up and down the aisles searching out chocolate treats.

"You want to come meet Alice and Peepsie?" Ziggy asked next, interrupting my dogs-on-a-plane thoughts.

The Twinzies and I nodded enthusiastically.

Alice and Peepsie, Ziggy's chickens, were happily clucking around a fenced-in part of the yard, unfazed by the excitable yapping and barking of the dogs. The chickens dipped their heads in and out of a feed tray.

"Here, Lena, you hold this basket. Let's go and see if

they've laid any eggs," said Ziggy.

The chickens' coop was made from stacked wooden boxes with material covering the front of it. "I like the chickens to have privacy. Give them some dignity when laying their eggs," said Ziggy. We all nodded in agreement.

Ziggy drew back the curtain to reveal two brown eggs nestling in straw. "Not bad. They've laid one each. But don't worry, we have more eggs in the house for cake baking." He gently popped the two eggs in the basket.

I looked again at the chickens pecking away. Would Alice and Peepsie wonder where their eggs had gone when they returned to their coop? They seemed to be the sort who got on with things and would just lay another couple of eggs tomorrow. I wish I could be as easy-going as a chicken. Wandering from one day to another not worrying about anything.

Just then, we heard Ziggy's front gate swing open. We had company.

THE GREAT CAKE-TASTROPHE

A boy, who looked around Ziggy's age, thirteen or so, jogged down the path.

"Wah gwaan, Zig-a-Zag?" said the boy to Ziggy.

"Yuh good?" said Ziggy in reply.

They both gave each other a greeting by flicking their thumbs across each other's thumbs, a bit like a fist bump, but which I found out later they called a "ding".

The first boy ignored me at first, nodding at the Twinzies. "You all right, Short Stuff One and Short Stuff Two?" he asked them, with a broad grin.

"These are my cousins, from England – Sunshine, Peter and Lena," explained Ziggy. "You three meet my friend Chef Beats — or Chef B for short."

I could understand him being called Chef as he liked to cook, but I didn't know where the Beats part of his name came into it.

"Ah, these are your baby cousins?" said Chef B. I shuffled in awkwardness. Also, who was he calling a baby? I could only have been a couple of years younger than him.

The boy seemed to pick up on my awkwardness and grinned even more. Looking directly at me, he burst into song.

"Don't be shy,

Just give it a trrrrrry,

I'm a bit much sometiiiiimes,

I ain't gonna lie."

Chef B held his hand passionately against his heart as he sang.

"Um, as well as cooking, Chef also likes to sing. That's why we call him Chef Beats — because he writes songs, too. If he doesn't become a chef, he might become the next biggest music star." Ziggy smiled.

That explained it. Chef Beats was a singing chef.

"Hello," I said, quickly, in a very proper way, offering him my hand to shake. As soon as I did it, I cringed inside. I mean, what year was this, 1952?

Chef B laughed. "All right, English," he said, bowing in the same way that Ziggy had done the previous day to tease me.

I don't have airs and graces, at least I don't think I do. I just didn't know how to act like an ordinary eleven-year-old in front of new people. Chef B had completely made me nervous.

"Bless and respect," said Chef B, after taking me up on the offer and shaking my hand. "You're as tall as your cousin. Trust me, we should call you Long Foot. Tell me something, Long Foot, what do you think?"

I shuffled from foot to foot, or should I say from long foot to long foot, and began scratching at my neck, which suddenly felt hot and itchy.

Ziggy picked up on this and made a wide-eyed gesture over at Chef B as if telling him to shut up. "Ahem, we should get on with baking before the big people come over. We've already collected the eggs."

Chef B clapped his hands together grandly. "Let's go! What do we want to bake? Belgian waffles? American cookies? French patisserie? Italian meringues? I've got cookbooks with recipes from around the world. Lay your requests on me."

The Twinzies giggled. Chef B certainly did have personality as well as recipes.

"Um, yes, well, we're arranging a wedding vows' renewal ceremony for my parents for their fifteenth crystal wedding anniversary. It's a surprise for my mum, so we need to keep it a secret. We were thinking about something closer to home like an iced Jamaican fruit cake," I said, regaining my composure and getting organized.

Chef B looked disappointed for a moment that we wouldn't be choosing one of his international recipes but then his face sprung to life.

"Let's celebrate crystal,

We'll make it taste like schnitzel," he sang.

As far as I could remember, schnitzel was a thin slice of pounded meat, covered in breadcrumbs. I hoped the wedding cake wouldn't taste like that. I gulped, wondering if Ziggy's teenage friend was the best person to make my parents' special anniversary wedding cake. But it was too late to change my mind. With sudden urgency, Chef B headed into the house. We all followed.

Big Dog, Lion and Rudie whined as they weren't allowed in the kitchen.

Miss Winnie looked at Ziggy and Chef B and sniffed. "You behave yourselves, you hear. I'm just going to do some ironing." Miss Winnie paused and looked back at us as she walked out of the kitchen. Ziggy smiled sweetly and Chef B waved her off merrily. Miss Winnie shook her head, chuckling to herself, and left.

Chef B was the conductor of the kitchen, and we were his orchestra. With a wave of his hands, we were ordered left, right and centre, to fetch ingredients: flour, butter, sugar. Lena and Peter cracked Alice and Peepsie's fresh eggs into the bowl, and Ziggy and I helped Chef B with the mixing. This reminded me of when Charley, Arun, Evie and I, as well as our classmate Riley, had baked a cake for our Year Six charity day with my Glammy Pepper. That was fun too.

Miss Winnie had allowed us to use the sultanas in a jar, which had been soaking in rum for months to add extra flavour into them. Granny Cynthie did this to her sultanas at home when she was preparing to make fruit cakes, too. We lifted the top off the jar and the pungent smell nearly knocked us out.

"Is it safe to use these?" I asked.

"Of course!" cried Chef B. *"You can't have a Jamaican wedding cake without fruits soaked in rum. Sunny, sunny Sunshine that would be soooooo wrong."*

He was singing again in that heartfelt way of his, where he puts his hands up to his chest, like an R&B singer. I couldn't help but stifle a laugh. He was growing on me.

Chef B sang merrily all the way through the baking — and then we helped ourselves to a snack of Jamaican crackers and cheese after we'd popped the cake in the oven. This was going so brilliantly well, we even had time to go on Ziggy's PlayStation.

Once the golden-brown cake was out of the oven, we needed it to cool before it could be iced.

"I kind of want to get this done today," I said, trying

my hardest to stay organized and on track. "We must go into town tomorrow to find a dress for my mum and then, the day after that, we're going up to Crooked Bend, to see the farm where my Grandad Bobby lived when he was young. And the whole family is coming over here later to see Lorna when she's back from work, so I don't want to run out of time."

Chef B nodded. "Okay, I know it's warm outside but let's leave the cake on the veranda to let it get some air. Hopefully, it'll catch a breeze. It might cool faster that way."

"Good idea," said Ziggy. "We can play a game outside while we're waiting, and keep the dogs with us so they're not tempted to touch it. I'm supposed to be giving my cousins a taste of authentic Jamaica, anyway, so it's all good."

This sounded like the perfect plan. We brought the cake out onto the veranda and placed it on a table with a mesh cover on top of it, to keep any insects away. The cake looked just like one of Granny Cynthie's special fruit cakes. It weighed a ton though with all those rum-soaked fruits in it. Still, Chef B had done a brilliant job. It was all coming together nicely.

"Let's teach them One, Two, Three, Red Light," suggested Ziggy.

"Yeah man, I haven't played that game in the longest," said Chef B, getting into the spirit of things. "I can do authentic Jamaica as well as international flair."

Ziggy explained how to play. "One person is 'it' and must turn their back, then they call 'one, two, three RED LIGHT' and turn around. The others, who are trying to sneak up on them, need to stop, without the person who's 'it' seeing them move. If the sneaker-uppers can sneak up without the 'it' seeing them in motion, then they win. If the person who's 'it' catches everyone out, then they win."

"Got it?" asked Chef B.

"Yes, it sounds a bit like What's The Time, Mr Wolf," said Lena.

Chef B decided he'd be "it" — the one to catch everyone out. With his cooking skills came bossiness, too, it seemed. He was like Gordon Ramsay without the swear words. I couldn't help but think that he would get on very well with

172

Evie. Or maybe they'd fight it out in a verbal battle to find out who would come out on top as the bossiest?

Chef B got most of us out in quick succession. Ziggy went out first, because Rudie had got overexcited and jumped onto him when he was trying to stay still.

"Rudie, why you always up in my face?" grumbled Ziggy. Rudie barked happily, thinking he had done well, and jumped up again, this time nearly sending Ziggy toppling over. "Okay, okay, I'll give you a treat. Now, please, STOP!" Ziggy chuckled.

Lion yapped even louder than Rudie had barked, so Ziggy gave him a treat, too. This triggered Big Dog, who started whining and making sad puppy-dog eyes. Ziggy gave her a treat as well, so that she didn't miss out. Ziggy was a big softie.

Lena went out of the game next. Then I tripped over a stone and flew with my arms propelling in front of me like a windmill to stop myself from falling. Chef B swung round and caught me in full falling motion. He howled with laughter. We all did.

But the person who took to the game like a duck to

water was Peter. He was a thief in the night, stealing steps towards Chef B and then, the next thing Chef B knew, Peter had tapped him on the shoulder.

Peter did the moonwalk, shouting out, "Oh yeah, oh yeah!" as he travelled backwards along the dusty ground.

"Gwaan, Likkle Pete!" laughed Ziggy at the top of his voice.

Rudie, Lion and Big Dog joined in with the celebrations. The chickens minded their own business and continued pecking at the ground. We looked across at Brian's pen.

He wasn't there.

Horror set into Ziggy's face. He swung round in the direction of the veranda. "OH NO NO NO — NO!" The rest of us looked over in the same direction — and then we all started running.

"No, Brian! STOP! STOP!"

I called as I ran.

Somehow, like
a magical, naughty
goat, Brian had broken

out of his pen and was trotting up the steps of the veranda towards the cooling cake. Brian stopped for a moment and looked around at us, as if he was considering our pleas, but then decided to ignore us.

As we got to the steps, Brian leaped like a great flying goat. His hooves extended gracefully into the air and pushed the cake off the table onto the floor. The cover shot off the cake leaving it exposed, but, miraculously, the cake landed on the veranda floor in one piece. We could save this situation if we thought quickly—

Nope, too late. The temptation was too much for Brian. He bit down into the cake, with his goaty mouth tearing a chunk straight out of it.

"No, Brian, no!" Ziggy wailed.

"My glorious cake!" howled Chef B.

Brian bleated and chewed as if he was saying, "Yum!"

"We can save this," I said, desperately. "He's only eaten a slice."

Ziggy, Chef B and the Twinzies gave me a side-eyed glance.

"You know, maybe we could save it," chimed Chef B. "I could cut away the bite mark and turn the cake into a horseshoe shape. Horseshoes are good luck!"

"And boy, do we need some good luck," said Peter, shaking his head as he and Lena tried to keep the dogs at bay.

"Okay, let's back Brian into a corner," I said. "Chef B, you can then sneak the cake away. Brian might not notice if we distract him."

Ziggy threw his hands to his head. "Do you know why goats have rectangular-shaped pupils?"

We all shook our heads.

"So they can see almost everything — in all directions! We wouldn't be able to sneak a crumb past him, let alone a mashed-up cake."

"Oh," I said. "Still, it's worth a try."

Ziggy shrugged. "Okay, let's do this."

176

We tried to back Brian into a corner in some kind of goat and kids' stand-off.

Ziggy approached Brian carefully, one small step at a time, and Chef B started singing a lullaby to soothe him.

"Hush little goatie, don't say a word. Chef's gonna bake you a better dessert."

Brian was having none of it. Only ONE cake would do.

Still chewing, his mouth churning like a cement mixer, Brian looked us in our round eyes with his narrowed, rectangular eyes and grunted as if to say, "BACK OFF, THE CAKE IS MINE!" He stamped one hoof and then charged towards all of us. We all jumped like goalkeepers out of Brian's path as he ran straight through the cake, before leaping back down the steps of the veranda.

More chaos ensued. Rudie, Big Dog and Lion obviously thought this was now an all-you-can-eat buffet. They dived in like seagulls on a bag of chips, tucking into the remaining stomped-on cake. We chased them off the porch into the yard with Brian.

The goat and the dogs ran around each other in circles,

as if dancing around an invisible maypole.

"Have the animals eaten too much rum cake?" asked Lena.

The animals did look merry. "Um, possibly," I said.

The veranda was a mess. Mashed-up fruit cake with paw and hoof prints stomped into it was everywhere. Miss Winnie ran out of the house to see what all the commotion was about. She threw her hands to her mouth.

"Lord have mercy!" she cried. "What happened to di cake?"

"The goat ate it," said Peter, plainly.

I held my head in my hands. This was a CAKE-TASTROPHE.

After that, Operation Clean Up began. We put Brian back, securely, in his pen, the dogs had an afternoon nap to sleep off the cake, and we swept the veranda clean to remove any traces of wedding cake.

I shook my head. "Why can't I get anything right?" I said to no one in particular.

Ziggy gave me a consolatory pat on the back. "It's not your fault. I told you, Brian has ways. He's like the Houdini of the goat world. And who knew he would love cake THAT MUCH!"

"Hoody-who?" asked Chef B.

"Harry Houdini, the famous escapologist," I said.

"Okay," said Chef B, nodding in agreement. "Nuh fret," he added. "Cooking is supposed to bring spice, though admittedly, maybe not this much spice."

"Sunshine, you flew across that yard like Shelley-Ann Fraser-Pryce!" said Ziggy.

I didn't mind being compared to one of the fastest-ever sprinters in the world. We gazed over at Brian, who bleated at us, clearly delighted with his day's work.

"Here's looking at you, kid," I shouted to him.

Me and my cousin and my cousin's friend looked at each other hopelessly and then burst out laughing. We couldn't stop.

"BIG PEOPLE — INCOMING!" called the Twinzies in unison.

A car horn tooted. The rest of the family had turned up to see how we were getting on. Lorna drove in right behind them.

179

"Are you behaving yourself, Badrick?" Great-Aunt Joy asked Chef B, using his proper name.

Badrick became as meek as a little mouse, not as showy as the Chef Beats I'd been hanging out with all day. "Yes, of course, Miss Joy." Great-Aunt Joy reached up and patted him on the head.

"What have you lot been up to?" asked Mum.

"Oh, just fun and games," I said with a shrug.

"We taught the twins and Sunshine a traditional Jamaican game," said Ziggy, covering over our tracks. "One, Two, Three, Red Light!"

"Ooh, I like that one," said Auntie Sharon, with glee in her voice. "Cheryl, remember when we used to play it?"

Mum smiled warmly. "Yes, I do. We played it with your mum and her friends, Ziggy, at your grandmother's house when we were younger."

"Let's have a game for old times' sake," said Auntie Sharon, delight lighting up her face. And with that, the grown-ups — Dad, Dennis, Auntie Sharon, Lorna and Mum, and even Miss Winnie — were off, playing the game like they were kids again. Ziggy, Chef B, the Twinzies, Daz and I joined in too. We thought they'd be out easily with them being so old, but they were tougher, faster and wilier than we'd given them credit for. My grandparents and great-aunt sat on the porch and howled with laughter.

"Yes, show the young ones how it's done," called Great-Aunt Joy.

"We old, but we're not cold," shouted Glammy Pepper.

And, you know what? Despite having no wedding cake to show for it, this turned out to be one of the most fun afternoons I've ever had. The dogs danced, the chickens clucked, and Brian the goat bleated his head off, thrilled with all the company and an unexpected treat of afternoon cake.

19

THE MARKET

The next day, it was time to go into the nearest large town to try and find Mum her surprise dress, for the wedding that was in exactly a week's time.

But after the excitement of the day before, I think all the grown-ups had overheated and were flailing with exhaustion. Plus, there was an additional problem.

The mosquitoes really were in love with Auntie Sharon. They had bitten her so much during the night that she had woken up with a giant swelling just above her ankle. Lorna had to go to the local pharmacy to pick up medicine for her. The supplies that Granny Cynthie had sent ahead in her barrel weren't enough.

"The game's up," said Auntie Sharon very dramatically, as her boyfriend, Dennis, bathed her forehead with a wet flannel. She was lying on the sofa. One of her hands hung limply, while she waved the other one about, throwing it to her head. "I can't make it into town to find the cake and the dress."

Auntie Sharon sank further into the sofa and closed her eyes.

"But no one shops like you," I howled. "You're the SHOPPING QUEEN!"

Auntie Sharon managed to acknowledge this fact with another vague wave of her hand.

"You've got that right," said Dennis, using the wet flannel to dampen his own head.

"I can't do it on my own. I can't do any of this without you," I told her. "I keep getting things wrong. The goat even ate the cake we made to surprise you all with."

Auntie Sharon opened one eye. "Pitfalls are all a part of life my precious niecey-weesey. But when you fall into a pit, you must use other resources to get yourself out of it. We'll get extra help. It's time to unleash the big guns. We need Glammy Pepper on the case to help with the cake and the dress. Besides, my blood runs through your blood. Admittedly, so does your mother's, with her lack of fashion sense, but we shall overcome. Go forth and prosper. Take my credit card out of my purse and buy the cake and the dress! Spend, spend, spend — let the credit card bend. I believe in you!"

Auntie Sharon closed her eye again, clearly exhausted after her stirring speech.

I thought about Mum and Dad on this holiday. The way Mum was beside herself with excitement at the sight of her favourite film star. Dad had even been getting himself fit in the hotel gym, in readiness for the big day. It was as if both of them were replaying their youth. I wanted everything to be right, but, so far, everything I'd touched had gone so wrong. Mum falling into the pool, the cake fiasco, Auntie Sharon getting sick — what disaster would strike next?

Still, Auntie Sharon had put her trust in me, so I had to try.

"I'll think of something," I rallied, patting at the stone in my pocket.

"Think of what?" said Mum, suddenly appearing from the kitchen with a tray filled with cups of cocoa tea.

"Erm, I was just saying that I'm really looking forward to going into town — and I'm thinking about what to wear." I crossed my fingers behind my back. I'd have to be careful that my fingers didn't get stuck together one of these days, with all the half-truths I was trying to get past Mum.

I mean no way did I really want to go shopping. It was far too hot, and I didn't fancy the bustle of busy shops. I wanted to be lying on an inflatable flamingo in the middle of a swimming pool at the Grand Beach Hotel or floating like a starfish in the sea. But there was a job to do. Quite a few jobs as it happens, before next week's wedding.

"Sunny, about that... Now that Auntie Sharon is poorly, and after yesterday's games' exertion, I feel like we should stay here and all rest up for tomorrow's trip up to Old Farm. Your dad's even having a bit of a lie-in. He's got so many aches and pains from spending all that time in the gym at the hotel. I've never seen him so enthusiastic about keeping fit." Mum laughed. "Anyway, I'm getting distracted. I don't want to tempt fate with any other problems. We really must get up to Old Farm to see Great-Aunt Vi tomorrow. I like a busy schedule as well as the next person, but how about we just chill today?" Mum smiled at me gently.

I said nothing. Mainly because I'd never heard Mum use the word "chill" before — apart from when she was talking about chilling things in the fridge — and it took me by surprise. What did Mum know about "chilling"? Also, I'd have to stop Dad from working out. He'd have to sit on the toilet or on the sofa, like a coach potato, reading his newspaper like he usually did, instead of keeping fit. Otherwise Mum would be on to him.

But I really needed to go into town to find a dress and to check out wedding cakes. The next day we'd be going up into the hills to visit Grandad's old farm. Chances were everyone would be too tired to go into town after the trip and then it would be time to go back to the hotel. I tried to think of an excuse that didn't involve any head tapping and an emergency rescue by the Twinzies. I couldn't. My hand moved towards my head.

Glammy Pepper stepped in and saved me.

"NONSENSE! If you old folks want to stay indoors and 'chill' then fine. I'll take Sunshine into town. It would be my pleasure."

Had Glammy overheard my conversation with Auntie Sharon? Did she know about the secret wedding?

"I'll go too!" said Ziggy. I hadn't heard him come in.

"And us!" chorused the Twinzies.

Even Daz said he'd come along for the ride — and be torn away from his phone and his beloved "she's not my girlfriend" Tiffany from Texas.

This was turning out better than I could have dreamed of. If we could go into town without Mum, we'd be free to do as much dress and cake shopping as we wanted. Glammy Pepper had excellent taste; she'd know what to do. And the rest of my family were right behind me.

"Right, oh, okay, then," said Mum, hesitating, but then relenting. Mum was letting go and letting us organize something for ourselves.

Auntie Sharon sat up and grabbed my hand before we left. "Good girl, the show must go on." Then she slumped back down onto the sofa, with a loud groan.

I breathed a sigh of relief as Glammy Pepper, the Twinzies, Daz, Ziggy and I got into the people-carrier taxi. But then a sudden twist of fate upended my plans.

"You know what? I think I might come along for the trip, after all," we heard a familiar voice call from behind us. I flung myself around in fright. It was Mum. "A girls' — and boys' — day out," she said. "How about it, Sunshine? We're on holiday, we need to make the most of every moment. No need to chill today." Mum swung her handbag over her shoulder and got into the car.

I WAS DOOMED.

My face crumpled like creased laundry. Mum was back into Mum mode. She suggested that, first, we visit the town's market so that we could "get a taste of authentic Jamaica" and then we'd walk around the main shops.

I cheered up a bit. Yes, the shops! That could work — but I'd have to find a way to get rid of Mum. Auntie Sharon had been doing her research beforehand and had told me there was a wedding-dress shop and a cake shop in the shopping centre. Ziggy had said he'd take me there, but also that he'd never had to buy a wedding dress or a wedding cake before, *"because I'm thirteen and why would I be interested in stuff like that?"* so he wasn't sure where those particular shops were. It was a fair point.

I nodded my head in determination. We'd find the shops, but first we'd have to ditch Mum. I'd just need to draw on the Twinzies for help, with strict instructions for them not to push Mum into anything — literally.

The town was **INCREDIBLE**. I'd never been anywhere like it before. It was busy and brimming with energy. The rainbow-coloured shops stood cheerily in yellow, dusty orange, green, red, blue and pink; the sound of people and their conversations filled the air; and car horns beeped for no other reason, from what I could tell, than the excitement of joining in with the hustle and bustle. It was hot — steaming hot — both with the bubbling atmosphere and with the soaring temperature.

We headed into the market. Sights, sounds, textures, tastes and smells all hit me at the same time, maxing out my senses. Stall after stall was jammed into the large space, and we dodged past people pushing handcarts piled high with yams, garlic and breadfruits.

One stall sold pots and pans. Another sold children's clothes. But it was the colourful food produce, in the heart of the market, that set the place alight, filling the air with a heady mix of scents. Nutmeg, ginger, cinnamon leaves and all-spice; multi-coloured scotch bonnet peppers, pumpkins, spring onions, pineapples, plantains and green bananas; avocado pears, cho-chos and watermelons. There were so many sights to feast on that my eyes danced in front of me, trying to take it all in.

My mouth watered as I watched a stallholder chopping tall, juicy sugar cane with a large knife. Ziggy said the knife was called a machete — or cutlass — and had to be managed with great care. The stallholder was so skilful with the sharp blade. One false move and he could have chopped off a couple of fingers along with the sugar cane. CHOP. CHOP. CHOP. SLICE. SLICE. SLICE. The sight was mesmerizing — and it reminded me of Grandad. He used to chop up the cane too into small pieces and we'd suck the sweet, sugary water out and then spit the pulp into a bowl, because you can't eat that bit. It wasn't a very pretty sight, but it was worth the ugly effort for that sweet, tasty sugary juice. I smiled at the memory. Glammy Pepper jolted me out of my sugary thoughts and asked if I wanted her to buy me some of the sugar cane. I shook my head. I don't know why, it just felt like a memory I wanted to keep with Grandad.

We moved on through the lively, buzzing market. Stallholders and customers shouted out as they sold and bought their goods, blurring into a symphony of blended sounds.

As soon as we walked out of the market, once Glammy Pepper had bought yams, green bananas and avocado pears for dinner, the sun's rays were back, vigorously beating down on our heads with a sticky heat. The canopied area of the market had kept us all a little cooler, but outside was HOT. HOT. HOT.

"Bwoy, the sun is sweet today. Whew!" Even Ziggy was feeling the heat's sting.

I found myself getting faint with thirst and weariness. But we still needed to hit the shops. I wished I'd taken up the offer of the sugar cane. But then the Twinzies noticed something that made their eyes light up as if they'd just seen an ice cream van. Instead, it was a man at a little cart with cups and containers.

"Who's that man, Glammy?"

"Oh, that's the sky juice man!"

Mum clapped her hands in delight like a big kid and said, "That was my favourite thing in the world when I was your age, I loved drinking sky juice. Now this is a piece of original, traditional Jamaica I couldn't get enough of!"

If this sky juice made cool and calm Mum have that

reaction, we had to try it. Glammy bought the sky juices for Ziggy, the Twinzies, Daz and me. The sky juice man used a shear which looked a bit like an ice skate to slice off shards from a huge block of ice. The sound SHUISH SHUISH SHUISH was hypnotic. He tipped the shards into four cups. They looked like snowy mountains. He squeezed lime onto the ice for extra flavour and then we all chose from strawberry, ginger beer and pineapple syrups to squirt on top of the ice.

"Strawberry is usually everyone's favourite," said Ziggy, "but I love ginger beer."

I chose strawberry (when in Jamaica do as the Jamaicans do), Daz chose pineapple, and the Twinzies chose a mix of all three flavours because that's the Twinzies for you — and then the sky juice man added some water to all of them to help melt the ice.

The drink was ice-cold, sweet and pure deliciousness in a cup; we slurped like it was the first and last drink we'd ever have. Mum had a little sip of each and savoured the taste, but then she decided to have some coconut water at a stall a little further on. A woman with another cutlass knife chopped off the top of the coconut and stuck a straw in it for Mum. I took a sip, even though I was unsure at first. Aside from having Grandad's sugar cane, I was only used to drinking things that came out of cans, cartons or cups, but the coconut water tasted cool, refreshing and sweet. I can understand why coconuts are a key part of life for people stranded on desert islands, like you see in films. I reckon I could live on coconut water for at least a month.

"I'm having such a good time, Sunshine. I'm so glad I came along. Thanks for inviting me," said Mum.

I nearly choked on the coconut water. I most certainly DID NOT invite Mum on this outing; she'd plonked herself in the car all by herself. But I was glad to hear she was having a fun time. I was happy for her.

"I'm glad you're here, too," I conceded.

Daz nudged me. "Don't we have a mission?" he whispered.

While Ziggy kept Mum busy by showing her more stalls outside the market, I had a secret word with Glammy Pepper.

"Glammy, I need your urgent help. Can you lead me to shops? Bridal and wedding-cake shops, in particular."

"What on earth?" muttered Glammy. "Who's getting married? Not Sharon and Dennis after a whirlwind romance? Very romantic, but surely far too soon—"

"No, Glammy, it's not Auntie Sharon. It's Mum. Dad's planning a surprise for their anniversary and we need to find a dress. I don't really have enough time to explain now—"

"No time to explain what?" Mum was on my shoulder like a nosey parrot.

A look of confusion was etched into both Mum's and Glammy's faces.

There was nothing else to do... I started patting my head. The Twinzies were at our sides faster than twin genies out of a lamp.

"After that drink we're SOOO hungry," said Peter.

"Yes, and my legs are SOOO tired after that LONG walk in the market. Can we sit down somewhere?" said Lena.

The Twinzies were really getting good at this trickery. Scarily good.

"Yes, let's take the children for some patties, while Daz and Ziggy and Sunshine explore a little more. They'll be quite safe," said Glammy. There was a twinkle in her eyes like she was cottoning on that there was a secret plot afoot.

"But aren't you three hungry too?" asked Mum.

Daz almost nodded, but I gave him a gentle nudge to the ribs.

"Ouch!"

"Daz means NO. We're absolutely not hungry at all in the slightest. Those drinks have really filled us up. And I just love this blistering warm air. Daz and I can't get enough of it. We want to walk around some more... Don't we, Daz?"

Daz didn't move. I gave him another friendly-ish nudge. Daz nodded.

Okay, I wasn't as slick as the Twinzies, but my wooden acting skills, miraculously, seemed to do the trick. Just about.

"Well, okay then..." said Mum, hesitation brimming in her voice.

"Off we go to the patty shop!" said Glammy, turning Mum on her heels and walking off in the opposite direction, before Mum had a chance to change her mind. Once Mum was a few steps away, Glammy turned around and walked back in our direction. "I'm sure Ziggy will show you the way to the main shopping precinct. There are especially good shops to browse towards the back end, on the right-hand side. Always good to find something old, something new, something borrowed, something blue." Glammy winked.

Hey, wasn't that an old rhyme people would say when someone's getting married? I think Glammy had worked out what I was trying to do. I grinned broadly. "Thanks, Glammy," I mouthed.

20

BEAUTIFUL BRIDES TO BE

Glammy was spot on. The bridal shop was right where she said it would be. It was next to an empty shop near the back of the shopping centre.

Daz, Ziggy and I stood outside the shop and gawped. It was like staring at a snowy, mountainous scene. Made from material.

White dresses were lined up neatly in the window, falling gracefully from clothes hangers, like a snowstorm in the middle of this tropical paradise.

"How are we going to afford any of these?" said Daz.

"I have your mum's credit card."

Daz glared at me — hard.

"She TOLD me to take it to buy a dress... Look, I don't have time for suspicion and doubting – and without Auntie Sharon or Glammy Pepper with me, you two will have to do. Let's go!"

A little bell rang as we walked into the shop. It was more of a gentle tinkle than an all-out wedding bell ring.

"Welcome to Beautiful Brides to Be. Can I help you?" asked a woman, dressed in a floaty summer dress, with a bit of a snooty voice. She was looking at us down her nose, as if her eyes were travelling along a steep ski slope.

"Um, we need a dress, please," I said.

"Visits to this shop are by appointment only," said the woman, whose nose had begun to sail into the air, lifted by her snootiness. "Do you have an appointment?"

I shook my head and my belly started to flip over. "Um...no."

I felt silly. What was I even doing in this shop?

I'm sure I heard her kiss her teeth quietly. "Are you the bride, groom and best man?"

"No! These are my cousins and I'm eleven. I need a dress for my mum. I know it seems unusual, but, you see, we're planning a surprise wedding vows' renewal ceremony for my parents. Well, more for my mum, my dad knows about it...it was his idea." I felt my mouth going into overdrive like a rolling, rambling river. "It's a really special time, because they'll be celebrating their crystal wedding anniversary. But my auntie's sick, so she couldn't come, and my grandmother is distracting my mum at the patty shop whilst we're here. The wedding's next week and I only have today to shop in town. PLEASE HELP US!"

While I gasped for air, the woman looked all three of us up and down as if assessing whether this was some kind of grand practical joke.

"Well, as it happens, I've had a cancellation, so I suppose I can fit you in for thirty minutes or so. But look here, pickneys, if this is a trick..."

"Yes! I mean NO, of course, no it isn't. I'm saying yes because I'm so grateful." I *was* grateful, and I didn't want to ruin this before we'd even started looking at dresses.

My cousins backed me up, both nodding, and Ziggy laid on that bright smile that could charm birds out of trees. The woman's haughty nose sailed back to earth, and she turned into wedding-dress-seller express.

"If it's a wedding vows' renewal ceremony, do you want to invoke memories of the original wedding day or do you want to go for evening dress glamour?"

I nodded my head at both options in confusion.

The woman, whose name we found out was Diana, sighed, clapped her hands and then whizzed into action, whipping out dress after dress to show us. "Let's just give you a variety to choose from, shall we? I take it you have her measurements?"

We all nodded again, though inside my stomach was doing somersaults. What measurements?

The first dress had swathes of white material tumbling to the floor, like a rolling avalanche. It was heavy too. Diana gave the dress to me to hold up to the mirror and I nearly fell backwards, knocked down by the weight of it. Both Ziggy and Daz held me up straight.

"Um, I think my Mum's first wedding dress was quite big with puffy sleeves, but—"

"But this seems to be extra-puff on speed dial," blurted Ziggy.

Diana shot him a look. He smiled again. Surely it was only a matter of time before that magical beam would fail him.

The next dress had less material but still felt more like Mum would be wearing an actual wedding cake than a dress.

The third dress was better. Still white but with fewer frills, and it didn't feel like it had lead weights sewn into the hem of it either. I held it up to the mirror. My cousins stood behind me. We tilted our heads, looking gormlessly back at our own reflections.

"Do you think Mum would like this one?" I asked them, unsure.

"Uh…don't know," they said in unison, shrugging.

"Oh, come on!" I was drowning in a sea of choices. "Daz – just imagine it's a tracksuit or that Tiffany is wearing it."

That was the wrong move. Daz twisted up his face into an ultra-mega scrunch. "Tiffany and I are just friends!" he huffed, with a force that I'd never heard from Daz before. I made a note to self to rein it in on the Tiffany-from-Texas teasing.

"Okay!" said Diana, chasing away the sudden dip in mood. "Let's try a different colour. Brighten things up a bit in here, shall we?" She took a deep breath before whirling like a tornado and dazzling us with dresses of assorted colours, shapes and sizes: racing red, garish green, popping purple (which reminded me a bit too much of my new school uniform). Short dresses, long dresses, in-between dresses. These dresses were made out of elegant silk, but I think, though lighter in the material department, they'd be too bright for Mum's bland plain tastes.

We shook our heads at each one. Diana's poor arms were moving like helicopter blades trying to find the perfect match.

I nearly fainted at the price tag of the dresses — they were as expensive as they looked. The more the shimmer, the shinier the price. But Auntie Sharon had told me to *"spend, spend, spend — let the credit card bend"*.

"Okay, what about this little number?" Diana was even more determined, faced with the challenge of finding the right dress. I felt hopeful. She reached into the rack of dresses and brought out a straight, strappy sparkly one. This dress looked a million dollars — literally — and it must have had a million and one sequins sewn into it too.

"Bwoy, I bet you can see this one from outer space, it's so bright," said Ziggy, shielding his eyes as if someone had shoved the actual sun into his face. I had started to realize something: Ziggy needed his big smile to compensate for his even bigger mouth. "Is that my reflection I can see in it?" he added.

I tried to stifle a giggle. Even Diana's lips twitched (in an upward direction not a downward one).

"My mum would like it," said Daz, deciding to speak to me again.

Daz was right. Yes, this would have been an ideal dress for Auntie Sharon's sparkly out of this world tastes, but this was Mum's big day not hers.

Daz's phone buzzed. "It's Glammy Pepper," he said.

"They've just about finished up in the patty shop and Auntie Cheryl is about to turn into a guided missile trying to find us."

I gulped. The wedding dress shopping had been surprisingly fun, but what had I to show for it except for double vision from the dazzling dresses and a bad back from the weight of some of them? I could make a desperation buy, but I knew in my heart that I hadn't found the right dress for Mum. It didn't matter how much money I could spend.

"We are so sorry for wasting your time. Thank you for trying to help us. I can't decide on any of these dresses. I don't think we're the right people for this job," I told Diana. I felt my shoulders slump, but that could have just been due to backache.

Even Diana looked as if she felt sorry for us. She cocked her head to one side and put one finger to her lips in thought. "You know, it can take brides months and months to find their perfect dress. It's no failure on your part. It's a tough job. You can get your mother a nice dress from a department store," she said soothingly.

I smiled weakly.

"You are really nice kids trying to do a good thing —
and that counts for a lot," said Diana. "Just make sure you
know her dress size *before* you go shopping next time,"
she added, one eyebrow raised.

I smiled properly now. That was a genuinely kind thing
to say. And helpful. But we were still leaving the shop
empty-handed.

"Can I help you with anything else?" asked Diana
before we left.

There *was* something else. "Is there a shop nearby that
sells wedding cakes?"

"Oh, there was a perfect one next door, but it closed
two weeks ago." Diana shook her head sadly. "Such a
shame. It wasn't getting enough trade."

My eyes prickled. Ziggy and Daz placed a hand each
on my shoulders.

"Come on, Cuz, let's go," said Ziggy. "We'll work on
something else. We're the 'A' team. Or more like 'B' or 'C'
team, when it comes to dress shopping — but that's still
a team." He winked at me.

I smiled at his silly joke. You know, the lack of dress and no cake may have been disappointing, but my cousins and I did feel like a team and that lit a spark in my heart.

"Good luck!" said Diana, waving us off.

"Thanks," I told her. "We could do with some."

21

THE GREAT JAMAICAN SEWING BEE

We arrived back at the house to the sound of a sewing machine buzzing away in the background.

Sailing above the busy hum was the racket of Great-Aunt Joy and Auntie Sharon singing along to the greatest hits of the singer Celine Dion. Great-Aunt Joy loves her, along with a country music singer called Kenny Rogers. They were both singing "My Heart Will Go On", the famous song from the movie *Titanic* at the (very) top of their lungs. My heart wouldn't have gone on any longer if I'd had to listen to much more of their singing.

"Is that you sewing, Joy? I thought you'd put the sewing machine into retirement?" said Glammy Pepper.

Great-Aunt Joy chuckled. "The people keep finding me. I'm just doing an emergency fix on this ripped pair of trousers for our neighbour. Can't have him going off to work showing off his behind, can we?" Great-Aunt Joy's piercing laugh ripped through the air.

"Joy was the best seamstress in town before she retired. She had people coming around asking her to mend or sew outfits for them from all over," said Glammy Pepper, proudly.

"Oh, that's nice," I said, starting to deflate after the epic fails of the wedding dress and cake, realizing that we were another day closer to next week's wedding.

When Mum popped to the bathroom to freshen up, I spilled the beans to Auntie Sharon and Dad. "I'm sorry. I've let you down. I've failed."

"K.M.T. KISS MY TEETH," said Auntie Sharon, kissing her teeth. "We're thwarted at every turn with these nuptials – but DO NOT WORRY."

"Ah, Sunny, you've done your very best and that's more than enough." But I could tell by the droop around his eyes that Dad felt disappointed.

Glammy Pepper was having none of the moping. "You certainly have not failed! Sunshine Simpson, what are you going to do when you find a subject that's difficult at your next school? Give in? No, when times are tough, do NOT give up," said Glammy. "Plus, you have help all around you. We will think of something."

Lena offered some light relief. "Great-Aunt Joy, do you think you could make clothes for Alice and Peepsie, and for Brian, in case they get cold at night?" she asked.

Great-Aunt Joy chuckled heartily. "My kindred twin, I've been asked to make many things, but never nightwear for some chickens and a goat!"

The thought of the animals dressed in their best pyjamas cheered us all up. And then it got me thinking...

"Great-Aunt Joy, have you ever made a wedding dress?" I asked her.

"Your Great-Aunt Joy can make anything," boasted Glammy, a knowing smile playing on her lips. She knew what I was getting at. "Come, let's talk," she said conspiratorially.

Five minutes later, Great-Aunt Joy was on board with

the secret, excitement dancing in her eyes at the challenge. She would make Mum's dress.

This cheered me up, but I was still cautious. I remembered Diana's advice in the shop.

"How will we get Mum's exact measurements for you to make her a wedding dress from scratch?" I asked. There was no way we could manage running a tape measure around Mum's particulars without her noticing – she'd rumble us in an instant.

Great-Aunt Joy looked thoroughly insulted. She straightened her back and held up her head. My great-aunt is one of the happiest people I've ever met, but for the first time since I'd met her, I noticed something different: the same fire and determination lived in her as it did in Glammy Pepper.

"My sweet Sunshine, I can accurately judge a person's measurements from one hundred paces, with a blindfold on. I changed your mother's diapers as a baby. I never forget a figure, no matter how grown they are. I know her inside out. This will be a piece of wedding cake."

Glammy Pepper and Great-Aunt Joy almost split their

sides laughing. What was it about twins, mischievousness and silly jokes? It clearly runs in the genes — well in our family's genes at any rate.

"And what about the wedding cake?"

"Well, I can't believe you didn't ask me," said Granny Cynthie, who was now looking insulted too. Even though I know Granny Cynthie is the best baker of cakes ever, I didn't want her to be worrying about this on holiday. But she was having none of it.

"By hook or by crook, I will bake the wedding cake," said Granny Cynthie determinedly. So, just like that, the wedding cake and the dress were rescued from the jaws of disaster.

As well as The Big Jamaican Bake Off, this was going to be The Great Jamaican Sewing Bee.

Here was the plan. While the rest of us travelled to the village of Crooked Bend to visit our relatives at Old Farm, Granny and Grampie would stay behind. They told Mum that the trip would be "too bumpy for their old bones". Granny Cynthie would bake the cake and Great-Aunt Joy would start working on Mum's wedding dress. She'd then finish the dress off after we'd travelled back to the Grand Beach Hotel. Great-Aunt Joy told us that she had material gathered from years of sewing to make it. She would deliver the dress and the cake to the hotel in time for the wedding. "That's a promise," she said.

I bit down on my lip, half in disbelief, half in hope. Could we really pull this thing off? Surely, it would be a mission even Tom Cruise might have found impossible, but with my family pulling together to help, it was worth a try.

22

ROLLERCOASTER RIDE

We set off into the hills early the next morning to make the most of the day.

Auntie Sharon, even though she was still hobbling on her swollen leg, decided she was feeling well enough to come. She said that singing the greatest hits of Celine Dion and Kenny Rogers — and then introducing Great-Aunt Joy to the sounds of Adele — had helped. (She had probably scared the mosquitoes away with her singing, too.)

Before we set off in a minibus taxi, Ziggy turned up with Chef B in tow.

"Wah gwaan? Everyting criss?" said Chef B. He was holding what looked to be a tray with a tea towel over it.

"What's that?" asked the Twinzies. We were all intrigued.

"I made croissants for your trip," he said, casually.

"No one knows croissants like me

People think they're patisserie.

They're not, they're from the family of Viennoiserie,"

he sang.

"Is this child all right?" asked Granny Cynthie, eyeing Chef B and his tray of croissants suspiciously.

"Yes, Granny," I giggled. "His name is Chef Beats because he likes to cook — and he likes to sing too."

"Oh, I see," said Granny, still looking at Chef Beats and his offering through doubtful eyes.

The Twinzies couldn't have been happier. They jumped up on Chef B with all the excitement and energy of Lion, Rudie and Big Dog, and nearly made him drop the tray.

"Hey, hey it was nothing, just a recipe from an old cookbook. No big deal," said Chef B. But I could tell he was pleased at the appreciation. His cheeks flushed.

We gobbled down the buttery, light pastry. These croissants were heavenly.

Grampie Clive gave Chef B a pat on the back, while Granny Cynthie chewed thoughtfully. Finally, Granny looked up and gave a nod of approval. "Delicious! Sunshine, how come you never tell me there's a new baker in town?"

Um, I'm sure that's what I'd told her ten minutes before, but anyway, Granny was so impressed with Chef B's skills that she invited him to stay to help her bake the cake.

"Really?" said Chef B, his eyes lighting up. "I hear you're a master baker, so that would be an honour. Thank you."

That praise pleased Granny no end. She practically adopted him as a long-lost grandson on the spot.

"Hey, we even have some fresh eggs courtesy of Alice and Peepsie," said Ziggy, revealing fresh eggs in his egg basket.

We left Great-Aunt Joy, Granny Cynthie, Grampie Clive and Chef B to do their thing. The rest of us set off on our trip up to Old Farm. Mum missed all our planning because she was already outside double-checking that the taxi driver knew where he was going. I shook my head. Mum just couldn't help but organize everything around her. Except the surprise of the century!

"Fasten your seat belts, it's going to be a bumpy ride," called Dad.

He wasn't wrong. As we drove out of town and the car climbed higher and higher up the green, but dusty, mountainous roads, the journey became increasingly 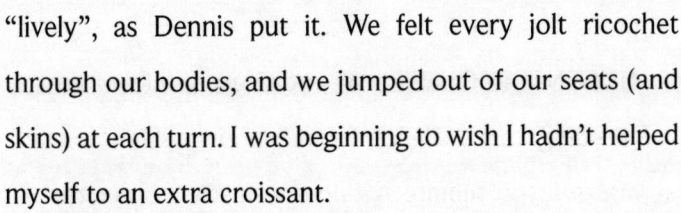 "lively", as Dennis put it. We felt every jolt ricochet through our bodies, and we jumped out of our seats (and skins) at each turn. I was beginning to wish I hadn't helped myself to an extra croissant.

"Wheeeeeeeeee! You were right, Mum, these roads are just like a rollercoaster!" trumpeted Peter, who was obviously enjoying the ride. And he's the one who complains he gets carsick!

Mum flinched before gripping onto her seat even tighter, and Lena was turning a bit green in the face. Luckily for Auntie Sharon, her medication had completely knocked her out. She slept through the entire journey. I'd never seen her so quiet.

A message flashed up on Auntie Sharon's phone. I was on high alert and turned to see who it was from: Miss Babette the wedding planner!

I sneakily took the phone to read the message in full. Auntie Sharon had given me her password so that if she was "conked out" as she'd put it, I could keep in contact with Miss Babette.

The message read:

URGENT REQUEST: We need to confirm the wedding meal. Please let me know which four courses you require ASAP. We need to order the food ingredients to ensure you have something glorious to eat on the big day.

Bon Appétit not Non-Appétit.

Regards, Miss Babette.

I didn't know what to do. Auntie Sharon was out cold. Obviously, I couldn't ask Mum for help, and it was too risky to try asking anyone else in the minibus. Mum's bat ears would be on to us in a nanosecond. I could wait to get advice from Chef B and Granny Cynthie when we'd got back from Old Farm, but that wouldn't be until evening. Miss Babette had said she needed to know details urgently. My brain flooded with too much panic all at once. If I didn't get back to Miss Babette quickly then, almost worse than having no cake, we'd have NO WEDDING MEAL. It was time to think fast.

It came to me. The people I always relied on to help me when I was in a fix were thousands of miles away, but at least I had my phone to communicate with them. I messaged Charley, Arun and Evie in a fluster. Being me, and my obsession with all things travel, I'd checked the time difference between Ireland and India before we'd left for Jamaica. I knew that County Cork was six hours ahead of Jamaican time and Gujarat was around ten hours ahead, so there was a chance they'd reply. I still wasn't sure where on earth Evie was on her cruise, so it was pot luck whether she'd answer. Evie has sophisticated tastes, ideal for planning a wedding meal, so I hoped she'd get the message at some point soon and get back to me.

Sunshine: HELP!!!!! What food would you want to eat at a wedding? Specifically, a Jamaican wedding with a very fussy bride.

Like the best friends they are, messages from Charley and Arun pinged into my phone within about ten minutes of each other.

Charley: What about chips? Everyone likes chips. Or sweets and chocolate?

Arun: What about something traditionally British? Try and do a creative switcheroo and bring Britain to Jamaica?

Sunshine: Ooh, those are good ideas. You can't get better than chips and I'll do a quick search for other popular British dishes.

Sunshine: It says here as well as chips, there's fish and chips, chicken tikka masala, a Sunday roast, sausage and mash, fish-finger sandwiches, and a full English breakfast.

Arun: Nice!!!

Charley: Well, there you go, menu sorted!

Hmm... I wasn't so sure Mum would be too pleased with some of those suggestions.

Ten minutes later, my phone pinged again.

Evie: Can't chat now, but just stick to something traditional. CAN'T GO WRONG!

I was torn between the things I thought might be nice, with the need to be traditional – but creative at the same time, just to pep the meal up a bit. This was SO confusing.

As Miss Babette was in such a hurry, I took Auntie Sharon's phone and replied to her with the choice that my friends and I had come up with. To cover all bases, I suggested she should "think traditional with a modern twist", listing the options. I also asked her to throw in something similar to the sky juices we'd enjoyed in the market the day before.

There was no further reply from Miss Babette, which, to be honest, after the hassle I'd gone to – disturbing my friends all around the world – I thought was a little rude. Still, at least that job was out of the way, and I'd given Miss Babette something to work with.

I soon put Miss Babette and all thoughts of food and the wedding meal out of my mind, because as we twisted and turned along the narrow, windy roads, up to Grandad Bobby's old family farm, I wondered if, somehow, we'd taken a wrong turn. Was there enough room on these roads for cars to drive along them? I dared not look out of the window too often, because, at times, we were driving very close to the edge of the slender roads, with a sheer drop down to the bottom of a steep ravine. I shuddered at the thought of the driver suddenly steering the car too far in the wrong direction.

"Nuh, worry," said Ziggy, noticing the anxiety etched into my face. "Not much further now. The driver's a professional, he'll have climbed these roads hundreds of times."

I glanced towards the driver, who was mopping at his brow with a handkerchief.

"I hope so," I said as we jolted over another bump.

Still, I managed a little smile to myself. These past few days had certainly been a bumpy ride, but surely now we were out of choppy waters.

23

OLD FARM

It was only another ten minutes or so before we reached our destination. We were high up in the hills, in the remote village of Crooked Bend in the River, or Crooked Bend, as it was known for short. Mountainous air blew across our faces, offering light relief from the piercing heat.

A little old lady (I'm not being rude she was SO tiny and old) came out of a small house to greet us. It was Grandad Bobby's sister, my Great-Aunt Vi.

"Glory be! How wonderful to see you all." Great-Aunt Vi is quite sprightly. She sprang over to the minibus like a gazelle on skates and gave each one of us a massive hug. Also, she may be old and tiny, but she has a very strong grip.

"Miss Vi, so good to see you," cried Glammy Pepper.

"And you, Miss Pepper," replied Miss Vi. "I am broken-hearted to have lost mi brother, Bobby, but I rejoice to see the rest of you all here with mi now."

I remembered how Grandad Bobby had always said he looked out for his sister when she was younger and that she would walk around behind him like a little chick following a hen. My English family had been able to enjoy his company for so many years; Great-Aunt Vi had Grandad for so few. My heart broke for her seeing the sadness fill up in her eyes.

We were all invited into the house. Miss Vi had decided she wanted to stay put in the original family home, which is where she still lived now. The rest of her family lived in a newer property further up the hill and kept an eye on her. We'd be going up to the bigger farmhouse for lunch later.

Looking around, I couldn't help but wonder – how did Grandad and his family fit into this small space? There was a tiny living room, sink and stove, and two bedrooms leading off it, with curtains for doors. One of the bedrooms was converted into a small bathroom to make things a bit more comfortable for Great-Aunt Vi.

"I remember, children, when your mothers visited here with your grandad and grandma when they were youngsters, they didn't want to use the latrine. It was outside. You had to walk down a little dirt track to get to it. 'Where's the toilet?' they asked. See it deh, I told them. I can tell you, they almost died of fright on the spot. Bobby had to drive them all the way back into town to use a latrine with a flush, because they wouldn't stop bawl. You called my latrine 'a never-ending black hole' if I remember rightly, Cheryl. You thought that something was going to fly out of it and bite you on your behind. It was nothing to fear, just a hole in the ground. All-natural stuff." Great-Aunt Vi threw her head back and roared with laughter.

"And they say *I'm* the diva," chuckled Auntie Sharon.

Mum reddened, shuffled in her seat and straightened her dress.

Then Miss Vi showed us a black and white photo of

her father — my great-grandfather — tending the farm, and another photo of a young woman standing in a field, holding a baby in her arms, with a young child next to her. I assumed the baby was Great-Aunt Vi and the young child had to be him. I'd recognize that square, ox-like frame anywhere. "Grandad!" I cried. "That's Grandad."

Great-Aunt Vi smiled. "I may not have many things, but many things I do not need. I have all I need right here — and these photos are my treasures." She held onto the photographs as if they were delicate feathers that might float away on the wind if she didn't tend to them with the utmost care.

"We can fix this place up even nicer for you, Aunt Vi. Maybe build you an extension or a new yard, so you have more room to spread out with your treasures," said Auntie Sharon.

Great-Aunt Vi shook her head and chuckled. "This place is where mi was born, and this is the place where mi will dead — and I wouldn't have it any other way. This new bathroom they built inside for me was enough. I couldn't cope with any more upheaval and dust. Modern life is overrated. Apart from YouTube, I quite like that." Great-Aunt Vi gave us kids a wink. Her eyes twinkled with mischief like Grandad Bobby's. "Come, mi will get your cousin Vernon and we'll both show you around the farm."

Great-Aunt Vi shuffled up to her feet and we went outside. She turned to look at me. "Ah, you have a smile just like Bobby's. You've made my heart sing."

All I could do was smile a little wider.

"Good girl, I bet he was proud of you," said Great-Aunt Vi.

"We were even prouder of him," I told her.

Tears sprung to my aunt's eyes. She reached up and patted me on the head. "Off you go now. I'm so glad you come visit me."

Miss Vi's grandson, Vernon, who's eighteen, joined us. He'd been working out on the farm but was happy to give us a tour. Everywhere we turned, lush greenery surrounded us. Up high, climbing towards the sky, were tall, green banana and breadfruit trees and, closer to earth, roots of sugar cane sprung from the ground, with sweet potatoes, wild yams and another vegetable called dasheen, growing all around. In fact, in every direction, all kinds of Caribbean fruit and vegetables were sprouting, from leafy callaloo and okra to medicinal herbs like wild garlic and turmeric. No wonder Grandad Bobby and Great-Aunt Vi were so strong if they grew up eating all this natural and organic food around them.

And then I saw it. A tall tree right in front of us, its branches bejewelled with red, orange and yellow fruit. Grandad's mango tree. I could tell in an instant. The mango trees in Great-Aunt Joy's garden stood together as a family, but this tree stood on its own: majestic, strong and proud, dominating the green landscape.

"Is that your special Number 11 mango tree?" I whispered awe-struck to Great-Aunt Vi, just so that she could confirm it.

My aunt stopped in her tracks and looked over at the tree. "Child, you know about di tree?"

"Yes. Grandad told me that you both used to climb it

and one day you didn't listen when he told you not to and you fell out of it and broke your arm."

Great-Aunt Vi rocked back on her heels, looked to the heavens, and let out a rolling peal of laughter. "Lord have mercy, you've brought me back seventy years," she cried. "'Pickney, your ears are too hard. Why you never listen? Today, I'll have to call this tree our Lucky Number 11 tree because you're lucky you didn't break your neck.' That's what Bobby told me." Great-Aunt Vi shook her head.

And then it came to me like a roaring wave. Grandad's lottery numbers. He'd used the seven times table for most of the numbers, but the number eleven was his special extra number. "Lucky Number 11!" I beamed.

"Come, it looks like the tree is as special to you as it is to me." Great Aunt-Vi led us all over.

Each one of my family held onto the tree's bark, closed our eyes, and felt its sturdiness, its roughness, its warmth.

"'Promise me you'll never climb that tree without me again,' that's what Bobby said. So, I told him, 'Cross my heart and hope to die.' And, from the day he left to sail to England, I never did climb this tree again. I couldn't, it would never feel the same — and I didn't want to break my promise." Great-Aunt Vi held back her tears.

"I'm sorry, Great-Aunt Vi. I didn't mean to make you feel sad by bringing up memories of the mango tree," I said.

"Sad?" said Great-Aunt Vi gently. "Yes, we mourn for the ones we have loved and lost. Yet, surely, we must rejoice in the joy they brought us when meeting them on their journey. And today, sweet Sunshine, you have filled my heart with nothing but joy. Memories are jewels. Hold onto them for as long as you can. They're too precious to let go of, even when time tries to steal them from your very grasp." Great-Aunt Vi stretched out her fingers and gave the tree trunk a gentle, encouraging tap.

Mum and Auntie Sharon got all weepy. I didn't know what to do but tap my hand on the pocket of my shorts. When I was unsure and didn't know what to do on this trip, I'd tap the stone in my pocket and feel comforted, as if Grandad was with me, helping me. But right there and then I knew exactly what I needed to do. I put my hand in my pocket and pulled out the stone.

I gazed at the black, gold and green stone and smiled.

"Great-Aunt Vi, Grandad painted this stone. I brought it with me on holiday to keep me company, but I think it belongs here. Grandad painted it in the colours of the Jamaican flag, so I guess it's come home. I'd like you to have it. It might be something to remind you of Grandad, just like it reminds me of him."

"Child, are you sure?" asked Great-Aunt Vi.

"Yes, just like you said, I still have my memories. Sometimes I think I don't know very much, but I'm absolutely sure about this. Grandad would want you to have it."

"Well, this gift is surely greater than gold. And I know exactly where to keep it."

Great-Aunt Vi took my hand gently in hers and placed it back onto the tree trunk. We traced our united hands around the bark, until we felt a small nook deep into the wood.

"Bobby would always hide secret treasures in here for me when I was a child so I could find them. He used to make me little toys made from wood that I played with so much I mashed them up. But this stone will never be broken. Come, put it in, put it in, it will be safe here always."

I suddenly felt wobbly, as if I didn't want to let go of the stone after all.

"You okay, baby girl?" Dad put his hand on my shoulder.

I nodded. My family gathered around me.

I shielded my watery eyes as I looked up through the tree branches towards the bright, blue sky. "I'm here, Grandad," I said, "I made it." Pausing for a moment, I tried to think of the right words to sum up exactly how I felt about being here.

"Do you see, Grandad? I'm on my very own adventure, like you told me to have, and I'm right here where it all began for you at your family farm. I couldn't come here without bringing you with me. I brought your stone home, Grandad. I must confess, I brought it here for me, but I'm going to leave this one with our Jamaican family and the sunshine-yellow stone will be in England with me, so you and I can be in both places."

Kissing the stone, I then tucked it into the nook of the

tree. "See, it's in very safe hands — and branches. Bye for now, Grandad."

"Come, let's give the child a minute," said Great-Aunt Vi. She scuttled away with the rest of my family. "Come, come there's more to see." Great-Aunt Vi ushered my family away like lost little chicks needing to find their way home.

Ziggy said something to me before being whisked away. "I hadn't realized you and your grandfather were so tight."

I choked up. "He was my best friend," I tried to tell Ziggy, with wobbly lips.

"Ah, that means he will always live in your heart. A bond of true friendship can never be broken. It's as solid as this mango tree."

I looked down at the ground, not wanting to seem like a baby in front of my older cousin and swallowed my tears. "Thank you."

Ziggy gave me a friendly punch on my shoulder and walked away.

Up at the bigger farmhouse we enjoyed a late lunch of soup made with the seasonal vegetables that we'd seen growing around us. It's a good job there was a bigger farmhouse. Two of Great-Aunt Vi's four children lived there, with their partners, and then there were six grandchildren, including Vernon, and two great-grandchildren. I enjoyed the afternoon playing with my baby cousins and chatting with my older cousins. Then we said our goodbyes before making the journey in the minibus taxi down the long sloping hill. It was just as bumpy on our way back but didn't feel as perilous – and somehow, I felt lighter, freer, happier.

Everyone else had fallen asleep, except for Ziggy, who sat next to me, and Dad and Dennis, who were sitting at the front, eyes peeled on the road.

"I know today was tough, Cuz, but are you enjoying yourself? In Jamaica, I mean," asked Ziggy.

"I'm having the best time, but today was hard. Selfish me almost didn't want to let go of that stone. I know it sounds silly…it's just an old stone."

"It's more than just an old stone. It means something

to you. And you did give it away. You didn't hold onto it. Even if you'd kept it that still wouldn't have been wrong."

I thought about this for a moment. Was Ziggy just being nice to me because he saw me about to cry earlier?

"Can I offer you some advice?" Ziggy waited for my reply just in case I decided to go into a huff or nudge him in the ribs.

"Sure." I nodded.

"I haven't known you for long, in person, but from what I've seen, you think hard on things. You don't just try to understand, you 'overstand' every situation, thinking too much about it. You're hard on yourself when you should just *be*. Your own worst enemy kind of thing. Don't worry about what other people think, just be yourself. Because you're safe, you're good, you're all right. It's been nice having my baby cousins here." He laughed then and I nudged him in the ribs and started laughing too.

"Ouch!"

"I'm so sorry! Did I hurt you?" I panicked.

"No. You're doing it again. Second-guessing yourself. You're fun to hang out with."

"Am I? Really?"

Ziggy nodded.

"I'm not sure the new people at school will think that. And what about if I can't do the work?" I heard my fears starting to spill out of my mouth for Ziggy to hear. "Sometimes everything just feels so wibbly wobbly. And just when you think you get the wibble right, everything wobbles again. Life doesn't seem to be straightforward."

I thought I saw Dad's head twitch and start to turn round, but then he kept his eyes on the road.

"How do you know until you try and get past the wobbles?" said Ziggy.

I shrugged.

Ziggy laughed. "Well, what do you like about your new school?"

"Well, I don't like the uniform, it's purple and I don't like—"

"I asked you what you *do* like. Focus on that for a minute."

"Well, the teachers seemed all right when we went to visit the school in Year Six for the open day. And I know we'll probably get to study Mandarin and go on geography trips. I like geography. And we'll play rugby and do some trampolining and other things I've never tried before."

"That sounds great," said Ziggy.

"But my friends won't be there — and I've known them ALWAYS and FOREVER."

"You know, I don't have all of the same friends as I did when I was younger. I have some of the same ones and different friends too. Remember, I told you, a bond of true friendship is never broken, no matter how far away you are from the people you really care about. You don't know something until you try it out — and your new school sounds pretty good. Plus, purple is a very regal colour."

I smiled at the memory of Mum telling me the same thing not so long ago about my new school uniform. "The school socks are nice," I said. "They're grey with little tassels."

Ziggy smiled. "Well, that sounds the best thing of all. Life's an adventure to be had. Go have it with your grey, tassely socks!"

I giggled. "My grandad always used to tell me to go

and have my own adventures, too. But nothing about socks with tassels."

"Well, your grandfather sounds like he was a wise kind of guy."

"He was. The wisest. And you know what, you're pretty wise, too."

"Hey, if you're calling me a wise guy, I'll take it," said Ziggy, smiling with that big comforting grin again.

I was so glad to have met my cousin. He was right: all the wobbly bits are just a part of life, and you have to work your way through the wibbles. There'd certainly been enough wibble wobbles with trying to organize the wedding – but I had realized something along the way. It had been fun too. High school might feel the same, if I gave it a chance.

We all tumbled out of the car back at Great-Aunt Joy's, just after sunset. I could hear the buzz of her sewing machine in the distance. Granny Cynthie and Chef B had managed to bake the cake. Chef B was going to take it home and ice it. He'd really won Granny over if she was going to let him do that without her watchful eyes on him.

Chef B smuggled the cake out of the house when Mum's back was turned, and we joined him in the garden.

"Long Foot English girl and Short Stuff One and Short Stuff Two, bless up yourselves. It's been good, yeh?" said Chef B.

"You sound like you're saying goodbye for ever. You are coming to the wedding, aren't you?" I asked.

Chef B's eyes opened wide. "*I'm* invited to the WEDDING OF THE YEAR?" he exclaimed, before Ziggy, the Twinzies, Daz and I hushed him. We made an even louder sound than Chef B with our united shushing.

"Yes, of course you are. You're our friend," Lena told him.

Yes, I guess he was. Chef Beats was our new friend — and I hadn't even noticed I'd made one.

"I'll be there," Chef B said proudly. "I wouldn't miss it for the world. Especially if your mum goes into the pool in her wedding dress!"

"Is that in the plan?" asked Peter in confusion.

"NOOOOOO! Definitely not in the plan! No one throws Mum into the pool in her wedding dress!" I said.

"Yeah, because if my Grandma Joy makes a dress as heavy as some of the ones in the wedding shop, your mum will sink like a stone," said Ziggy, shaking his head, before we all burst out laughing.

We took a selfie then: me, Ziggy, the Twinzies, Daz and Chef B. I smiled brightly for the camera while the boys tried to look super-cool, which made me smile even more. This photo was one for our family photo album at home.

I really liked my cousin and his friend — and that made me realize something.

I wasn't so bad at making new friends after all.

24

STORMY WEATHER

We spent the next day over at Ziggy's house, playing with the dogs, having a game of PlayStation and more Jamaican outdoor games. Ziggy's mum, Lorna, had taken the day off work, so the adults all chatted away on the veranda, as if no time had gone by at all since they'd last seen each other.

We travelled back to the Grand Beach Hotel the following day.

The Twinzies were allowed to go back over to Ziggy's house to say goodbye to the animals. Peter and Lena were both in floods of tears as they hugged Rudie, Big Dog and Lion, and patted Brian on the head.

"We'll save you a slice of cake," the Twinzies told Brian before running after Alice and Peepsie to stroke them. The chickens gave a dismissive nod of their heads and continued pecking at the ground.

"I can't leave them. I'M OBSSESSED," cried Lena, which drew stifled giggles from the grown-ups.

"Mum and Dad, I think we definitely need to get a puppy — and we need to have at LEAST two goats," said Peter.

"Yes, goats need friends, you know," said Lena, in a very matter-of-fact way. Mum and Dad both stopped their giggling and looked at each other in horror.

"Let's talk about it when we get back to England," said Dad, finally ushering the Twinzies into the car. We said our goodbyes to Lorna and Miss Winnie. "We'll see you in four days' time at the wedding," Lorna whispered to me.

I tried to take a last-minute photo of all of us together, but then Rudie decided he wanted to be in it too. He jumped up and photobombed the shot.

"Rudie, you're too rude!" we all cried. He barked happily.

Rudie and the other pets

would be one of my all-time best Jamaican memories.

Ziggy came back with us to Great-Aunt Joy's house so we could say farewell, for now, to her. She'd be delivering the wedding dress to the hotel on the morning of the wedding. It was cutting it fine, but Great-Aunt Joy needed the time to finish her sewing.

The whir of the sewing machine stopped, and she came out of the house to greet us, so that Mum wouldn't come in and see the dress.

"Is everything okay?" I asked as discreetly as I could.

"Don't worry, everything will be just fine." Great-Aunt Joy smiled and clenched one arm in a strong woman pose to show off her muscles. "Jamaicans have stamina and speed. I'll have that dress sewn quicker than you can say 'kiss mi neck'. But do me one small favour?" Great-Aunt Joy asked with a twinkle in her eye.

"Anything," I told her. She deserved it.

"Remind your Auntie Sharon to send me that Adele CD as soon as she can when you get back to England."

Ziggy put his hands together in prayer and gave a silent, pleading cry of "NOOOOO!" behind his grandmother's back. Great-Aunt Joy must have eyes in the back of her head, or rectangular ones like Brian the goat, because she spun round and caught him in the act. She gestured to swipe him with her tea towel, which sent Ziggy running around the garden in tears of laughter.

"Don't worry, Grandma, I love your singing. And don't forget, God loves the crows too!" he shouted from a safe distance.

"You see you, bwoy. Are you telling me I sing like a crow? You wait until you come back in this house today." Great-Aunt Joy chuckled and went back to the veranda.

"Bless up. Keep strong," Ziggy said to me when we had both stopped laughing.

"You too," I told him and gave him a quick awkward hug before getting into the car.

Glammy Pepper was joining us at the hotel for the final week of the holiday. She bundled a couple of suitcases into the minibus.

"We're only at the hotel for another week, not a month!" said Mum.

"Cheryl, I travel with outfits to match every occasion.

And you never know when something special might come in handy." Glammy's eyes glistened with mischief, just like her twin sister's minutes earlier. I tried not to smile in case I raised Mum's suspicions.

As the minibus moved off, we all turned to look out of the back window as Ziggy and Great-Aunt Joy, framed in a perfect picture by the mango and guinep trees, waved their goodbyes. For now.

I'd settled in quite comfortably at Great-Aunt Joy's with her family, the singing crickets, lizards, Brian, and the rest of the animal kingdom keeping us company, so it felt kind of weird to be travelling back to the Grand Beach Hotel.

I couldn't quite believe how the holiday had been zapping past in a flash. Part of me had been anxious about how I would find Jamaica after building up my hopes and dreams of travelling and having my own adventures for as long as I could remember, but this was something else: exciting, thrilling, overwhelming, tearful — all kinds of emotions, some of which I was feeling at the same time. I thought about my conversation with Ziggy, feeling wibbly wobbly about stuff. Maybe that's just how life is when you're experiencing something new or making new friends? It's like an obstacle course to work your way through. Sometimes the obstacles you must climb over come easily and sometimes they take a bit more effort.

I took out my notebook and looked at my list of things to do for the wedding.

The wedding cake was baked, and Chef B was going to put the icing on.

Great-Aunt Joy was busily working on Mum's dress.

I'd sent through the wedding meal choices to Miss Babette. She hadn't come back to me, so I took it everything was okay and on track.

We had guests. Wonderful guests. Great-Aunt Joy, Cousin Lorna, Miss Winnie, Chef B, Ziggy, Dad's family, who'd be joining us next week, and all our family from the big farmhouse, except one. I'd invited Great-Aunt Vi, but she said she'd been on her mountain for so long that she might "disappear in a cloud of smoke" if she left it. I felt sad that she wouldn't be there, as she couldn't make it to

Mum and Dad's first wedding either.

My mind then turned to Charley, Arun and Evie. I would have loved for them to be there on the second wedding day too, but at least they could still be with me virtually.

But now wasn't the time to get distracted. We just had to keep the ceremony a secret from Mum until the morning of the wedding. She would be so surprised that we'd been able to pull this off by ourselves. (We wouldn't need to tell her about all the hitches along the way.)

We were nearly there. But not quite…

As I gazed out of the minibus window and across to the far-off hills, I noticed the sky becoming an increasingly deeper shade of brooding grey. Stormy weather was on the way. I hoped this wasn't a sign of things to come.

"Are you okay, Sunny?" Mum smiled at me in that soothing way she does when she senses there may be something wrong.

I nodded and continued looking out of the window at the moody sky. Rolls of thunder peppered the air, as though they were the rumbling tummy sounds of a hungry dragon.

As the taxi pulled into the hotel, the clouds decided to unleash the dragon's fury. I'd never seen anything like this rain,  not even on the wettest days in England. The raindrops pounded heavily, falling like shooting arrows. But the rain's lashes were warm, like a dozen power showers hitting your skin at once.

We dried ourselves with towels given to us by the reception staff. The rain had soaked us to the skin in just the few yards we'd run to the hotel, and we watched from the balcony at the back of the lobby as the raindrops danced through the tree branches, and the ocean roared with foamy white waves.

The weather held us in a trance, but as quickly as the rain had come, it went, almost fooling us into believing it had never happened. The rolling blue sky made a comeback, bringing the hot sun with it and sweeping the storm clouds away, drying everything in an instant. Everything felt calm again, but then a new storm blew in...

Miss Babette ordered Auntie Sharon and me to go to her office once we'd settled back into our rooms. She was a little worked up as she'd been trying to contact Auntie Sharon and Dad but hadn't been able to reach them. But why? I thought everything was under control. Had I missed something off my list?

"Brace yourself, Sunny Sunshine, but don't worry about a thang," came Auntie Sharon's rallying cry. "Besides, I have more surprises up my sleeve. Nothing keeps Auntie Sharon down for long, not even those pesky mosquitoes."

I smiled. Auntie Sharon, even though she is undoubtedly the Queen of Chaos, always has a way of making the sun shine through the rain. Still, we brought Glammy Pepper along with us for backup, just in case things got rough. I think Auntie Sharon was as scared of Miss Babette as I was.

"Weeeeeell," said Miss Babette, extending and hanging onto the word for as long as possible. "This wedding really is something else."

"Thank you," said Auntie Sharon.

Um, somehow, I didn't think Miss Babette's comment was meant to be a compliment.

Miss Babette sat at her desk, tapped her long fingernails together and then reeled off the issues. "My dears, there is an invisible bride, a barely-made dress — which my sources tell me is at large in another part of the island — an impossible to contact chief bridesmaid, and an eleven-year-old junior wedding planner who has suggested chips, curry, something called fish-finger sandwiches, and a full English breakfast for the wedding banquet. This is, at best, unconventional."

"What can I say?" replied Auntie Sharon. "I'm not a very conventional kind of person and my niece is extremely creative — she thinks out of the box. And her suggestions sound lovely." Auntie Sharon smiled at me and squeezed my hand.

"Mizzzzz Williams, we try to accommodate every need — that is what we are here for. To make dreams come true. I am in no doubt that you and your niece have the best intentions, but you really are pushing things to the wire.

I hate to say it, but I am not sure this is going to work out."

Tears that had come as quickly as the rain filled my eyes. The way Miss Babette was speaking it was as if the surprise crystal anniversary celebration was the stuff of nightmares, rather than what dreams are made of.

Glammy Pepper, who up until that point had been uncharacteristically quiet, sat forward in her seat and patted me on the knee. She straightened her back and sat very prim and proper before she spoke, raising her chin and holding her head regally in the air. "Miss Babette, are you not Jamaican?"

Miss Babette was caught off guard for a moment. She nodded, cautiously.

"Well, let me share a Jamaican proverb, you will know all too well: 'when visitors come at wi fireside, wi meck wi pot smell nice'. We will always show our best side to others. No matter how dreadful things may seem, we always find a way to make it good — and we treat our guests with care."

Miss Babette pondered this for a moment and then replied. "Well pudding can't meck without fiyah. I need to have the right tools to make it work!"

I think Glammy and Miss Babette were having some kind of verbal stand-off, like a rap battle, Jamaican style. Glammy was saying when things get tough, we must pull together, and fake it till we make it. But Miss Babette was saying that she didn't think this whole thing was going to work out, because she didn't have enough to work with.

I felt I had to speak, before either of them said something that would cause the whole wedding to be called off. It was worth a shot.

"Miss Babette, I'm sorry that we haven't been as on-point as we should have been with the planning of the secret wedding. But we really have been trying SO hard. Now we're all back here in the hotel, can we work together to try and make it better? My mum always says that there is no substitute for experience – and you are both incredibly wise." (I added the "incredibly wise" bit so that both Miss Babette and Glammy Pepper didn't think I was calling them old.) "Auntie Sharon and I both need your help and brilliant-ness to make this work."

Miss Babette's mouth softened from a thin, hard line into a gracious half-smile. Glammy Pepper beamed, showing off her sparkling white teeth and put one arm tightly around my shoulder.

"My dear, you certainly have heart and spirit: a true Jamaican through and through, mi see it, yes!" declared Miss Babette. "COME, from the jaws of disaster we will rescue triumph! We shall not be defeated!"

"Nuh mug nuh bruk, nuh coffee nuh dash weh," chimed Glammy Pepper.

"Huh?" I said, completely baffled.

Auntie Sharon cackled. "It means if the mug isn't broken, nothing has spilled out of it, so no harm done." I was still confused.

Auntie Sharon grabbed my other shoulder (the one that Glammy Pepper wasn't grabbing). "I think your glamma and Miss Babette fancy themselves as Jamaican poets, like Louise Bennett-Coverley. What these absolute babes are trying to tell us is, IT'S SHOW TIME!"

25

SURPRISES

The next couple of days leading up to the wedding were a whirlwind of activity.

Everyone in my family, along with Miss Babette's hotel team, pulled together to make sure everything was ready. Poor Dad was tortured by Mum's constant hints in her last-ditch tries to get him to remember their crystal wedding anniversary.

"It's a crystal-clear day again, isn't it?"

"Are those crystal glasses at the dinner table?"

"Ooh, the sea is as clear as crystal."

But Dad wasn't biting. He was getting really good at ignoring Mum.

Auntie Sharon had decided she wanted to arrange the flowers for the wedding herself, using the skills she had learned on a flower-arranging course. Glammy Pepper rallied Great-Aunt Joy over the phone to make the last touches to the dress. And Grampie Clive and Daz helped the hotel staff with decorating the reception room where we'd be eating our meal, with golden streamers and lanterns.

Even the wedding meal finally came together — and, you know what, some of my ideas did make it onto the menu. Dad gave it the final seal of approval.

APPETIZER

Mini saltfish fritters and ackee and saltfish vol-au-vents

STARTER —

Red peas soup served with bread rolls

MAIN COURSE —

Jerk chicken / Jamaican escovitch fish (with spicy onions, peppers and pimentos) / vegetable curry,

served with white rice, rice and peas, and/or salt and
pepper chips, with a medley of seasonal vegetables
DESSERT —
Mango cheesecake, served with cream or ice cream
An assortment of candies (sweets)
Sky juice cart — with a variety of flavoured syrups

Basically, a whole load of **DELICIOUSNESS!!!!**

And then I got the greatest surprise of all.

A day before the wedding, Auntie Sharon dragged me from the swimming pool and into the hotel lobby. I'd been enjoying myself splashing around with Tiffany from Texas and Daz.

As I dripped across the lobby, wrapped in a towel, two familiar figures came into view at the reception desk. My Godmother Patsy, Mum's best friend — and Mrs Turner!

Auntie Sharon wanted to surprise everyone and had arranged to fly them over for the wedding.

"I couldn't let the old goat miss out on the wedding of the year, could I?" whispered Auntie Sharon, nodding over at Mrs Turner. "And I don't mean Brian the goat, either."

I stifled a giggle. "Auntie Sharon, you are awful, but also the kindest BESTEST auntie in the whole world." I gave her a massive hug and then galloped over to the reception desk and hugged Godmother Patsy and Mrs Turner too.

"Sunshine Simpson, you're getting me all wet," complained Mrs Turner. "You go from one chaos to another, you really do. But I must say, oh how I've missed your antics at home. It's been so boring without you." Mrs Turner grabbed me tightly and hugged me back.

There was another surprise…

Feeling a tap on my shoulder, after Mrs Turner had released me from her grasp, I turned to see a familiar bob of red hair and bright blue eyes peering at me.

"CHARLEY?" I cried. "CHARLEY, it's you! …Is it really you?"

I gave her a little poke on the shoulder, just to make sure she wouldn't disappear in an instant like the rain had done a few days before. But she was still standing there, looking like Charley and smiling like Charley. I was so beside myself with happiness, I managed to pick her up and swing her round in a circle.

"But how?" I shook my head still not believing who I was seeing.

"Your Auntie Sharon made it happen. When we got back from Ireland, she arranged for me to fly over with your godmother and Mrs Turner. It was impossible to get Arun here, of course, as he's still at the wedding in India, and Evie is somewhere out there in the world on her cruise. I was sworn to secrecy not to tell you. Even though it's the hardest secret I've ever kept."

"It's the BEST secret EVER," I called. "Apart from the wedding, of course." I smiled sweetly at Auntie Sharon — and she grabbed us all in for a group hug.

It was a glorious, perfect moment.

And then it all went a bit wrong.

With all the commotion and excitement in the lobby, we hadn't seen an extra person walk in.

"WHAT ON EARTH IS GOING ON?"

Mum had appeared from out of thin air, confusion set into her face. We'd all been caught red-handed.

"Patsy? Mrs Turner? Charley?

"How?

"Why?

"What?"

I had questions too, like WHERE had Mum sprung from and WHEN could we get rid of her? This was NOT THE PLAN. She wasn't supposed to know about the wedding until the next morning – on the day of the wedding ceremony and her anniversary itself.

Dad screeched into the lobby like a bewildered giraffe running in behind her. He face-palmed himself. "Sorry," he mouthed to Auntie Sharon and me.

There was only one thing to do. I started patting my head. Amazingly, the Twinzies, as if powered by instinct, arrived with Granny Cynthie and Grampie Clive in tow. But it was no use, the game was well and truly up.

"Can someone please explain to me what is going on? And Sunshine why do you keep patting your head at random moments?" demanded Mum.

"Fair enough," said Auntie Sharon. "It's all going belly up, anyhow. Now's as suitable a time as any to tell you… You're getting married in the morning."

"I'm getting married in the morning," echoed Mum in disbelief. "I'm GETTING WHAT?"

"Well, actually, you're getting married at two o'clock in the afternoon," I said.

Mum looked at me, her mouth wide open in shock or horror – it was hard to tell which one.

Mum then looked at Dad. "Tony?"

Dad shrugged, not knowing what to say to the woman who liked to be in control of absolutely everything.

"Um…isn't it all crystal clear?" he asked with that goofy expression on his face that Mum usually loves.

But her face didn't move. I decided it was time to try and save Dad's life.

"Let me try to explain, Mum. Please don't get bossy until I do." I don't think that helped. Mum's eyes bore into my soul. "We wanted to do something nice for you, as you and Dad have done so much for us, for literally our entire lives. This whole thing has been Dad's idea. He kept pretending that he'd forgotten about your crystal wedding anniversary, so that we could arrange a surprise wedding vows' renewal ceremony for you here, in the hotel. He wanted it to be special because last summer was really tough, when we lost Grandad, and because your original honeymoon had been so rainy. And Auntie Sharon has flown in all these special people to share in tomorrow's celebrations."

Mum looked at each of us, one by one, as if she'd never seen any of us before in her life, and then she did a very un-like-Mum thing. She burst into tears.

"Chez, don't cry, we can call the whole thing off. We don't want you to be stressed out about it," cried Auntie Sharon.

Mum dabbed at her eyes with the back of her hand. "No, no, no! I think this might be the kindest, most beautiful thing that anyone has ever tried to do for me. Thank you... Tony, I thought you'd forgotten."

Dad smiled his goofy smile again. "NEVER!" (Well, that was only a little bit untrue.)

"But what can I wear?" said Mum, hope and excitement beginning to ring out in her voice.

"We have a dress, but it's arriving tomorrow," said Auntie Sharon. "Aunt Joy is making it, so don't fear, you know it will be on point. Aunt Joy is the best!"

"Oh, I see," said Mum, thoughtfully, still processing all that she'd been told. "Well, even if there was no dress at all, I would wear a bin bag if that was necessary. Though I'm sure I could find something in my luggage that would be more than suitable."

Auntie Sharon frowned in disappointment at the thought of the outfits in Mum's suitcase. She and Mum have quite a different sense of style.

I was in contact with Ziggy later on that evening just to check that Great-Aunt Joy was all right. "Grandma's sewing machine is running faster than Usain Bolt to finish that dress. And we all have to pray she finishes soon, to stop her from singing the greatest hits of Celine Dion. There's only so much more we can take," he cried.

"Your cousin is funny," said Charley after I'd finished the video call.

"He is! I can't wait for you to meet him," I said.

26

CASPER THE GHOSTS

At breakfast the next morning, while we waited for the dress to arrive, I excitedly showed Charley the choices of what we could eat. She had hash browns, fried plantains (which she loved), scrambled eggs and a bit of steak, followed by waffles and orange juice. We giggled as we had a competition to see if she could stack her waffles higher than my stack of pancakes.

Glammy Pepper swept into the dining room; she had news.

"Darlings, don't panic," she cried, which made us all instantly panic.

"Oh, for goodness' sake, what is gwarning now?"

exclaimed Auntie Sharon. "Even I can't take much more of this excitement."

"You're telling me!" said her boyfriend Dennis, mopping at his head with a table napkin.

"Well, the minibus carrying the dress, Joy and the others has broken down on the highway. We don't know if the dress will make it to the ~~church~~ hotel on time."

Auntie Sharon let out a piercing cry of "ARGHHHHHHH! NOOOOOOOO! URGGHHHHH!" This may have been because of the broken-down minibus, but it may also have been at the thought of Mum plucking one of her own dresses from her suitcase to wear instead.

This wasn't good news. It wasn't just the dress that was somewhere stranded on a highway between Clarendon and the Grand Beach Hotel, it was the wedding cake as well — and, more importantly, most of the guests. I only had to hope that Brian the goat hadn't broken out of his pen and found his way into the minibus, otherwise the cake would have no chance of making it at all.

Mum looked Auntie Sharon square in the face and

said, "CHILL, sis" — which, to be honest, took everyone by surprise.

And then she turned back into Mum again, taking control of the situation. "We must NOT panic. If the dress is meant to be here, it will be here. In the meantime, we need something to calm our thoughts. Sharon, fancy a trip to the hotel spa?"

Auntie Sharon nodded.

"Well, what are we waiting for? Let's go chillax," said Mum.

Something strange was happening to Mum on this holiday, and I liked it!

Off we went to "chillax".

Mum, Auntie Sharon, Glammy Pepper, Charley and I enjoyed a pampering session in the hotel's beauty rooms. We all wore white dressing gowns and looked like ghosts as the beauty therapist slapped white stuff on our faces that was supposed to do "wonders for the skin" and had "anti-ageing properties". If that was true, by the end of the day I expected to look like a newborn baby again.

But the best bit was having our nails painted. We all

had matching golden toes and fingernails. I hoped the rest of the day would turn out to be this much fun. We could live without the dress and the cake. I realized it was the people I wanted to see again, my relatives and new friends.

Glammy's phone started ringing.

"Get that for me, will you?" said Glammy to no one in particular.

No one else moved from their chillaxing, so Charley and I scrambled to find Glammy's phone. It was in her dressing gown pocket. Glammy was lying flat on her back, her face still covered in white cream with two slices of cucumbers slapped over her eyes. Because Glammy had just had her nails manicured she didn't want to hold the phone either, so I rolled my eyes and put it on speakerphone for her.

"GLORY BE, sis! We're on our way! This blessed contraption of a minibus is fixed, thanks to a passing mechanic and the wonders of mango cupcakes!" Great-Aunt Joy exclaimed from the other end of the line.

Glammy Pepper sat bolt upright like a ghostly mummy, arms and legs outstretched, with the cucumbers still stuck to her eyes.

"We should be with you by noon at the latest! And bwoy, do I have a surprise for you all!" cried Great-Aunt Joy.

"Woohoo!" shouted Auntie Sharon, fist-pumping the air.

"Did your aunt say something about mango cupcakes?" whispered Charley.

I shrugged. "It's probably best not to ask, but if anyone can fix a car with a mango cupcake, it will be a member of my family."

But what had really intrigued me in that phone call was the talk of another surprise.

"What are we waiting for? We've got a wedding to slay!" trumpeted Auntie Sharon.

Auntie Sharon grabbed Mum's and Glammy's hands, cucumber slices flew in all directions, and they all bolted out of the therapy room, still in their dressing gowns and their faces caked in white. They ran through the hotel reception and up to their rooms like three Casper the Ghosts, with Charley and me following them, nodding and apologizing to everyone that had flung themselves out of their way.

THE DRESS

The dress — and the wedding cake — arrived at noon on the dot, accompanied by a guard of honour: Great-Aunt Joy, Ziggy and Chef B. When the call came through that they'd arrived, I bolted down to reception to greet them.

"Thank you so much, Great-Aunt Joy," I said, running over to her and giving her a massive hug. She looked tired but happy.

Great-Aunt Joy wiped at her brow with the back of her hand. "Whew! That was close!"

Ziggy was cradling the dress in its garment bag and Chef B held the cake box carefully.

"Is the cake all right?" I asked.

"Yep, no animal teeth marks in sight. At least the last time I checked," said Chef B. "But the two-dozen Number 11 mango cupcakes I baked early this morning didn't make it. They got eaten on the way here — mainly by the mechanic who helped us out on the toll road. He ate six of them as payment on the spot!"

I did a quick calculation. "You ate all the rest? Those cupcakes must have tasted good!" I exclaimed.

"Not just us. The others as well," said Ziggy. "We all got hungry waiting around so long to be rescued." Ziggy gestured over to the main door.

Recognizable faces flowed into the lobby area: Cousin Lorna and Miss Winnie of course, and our cousins from Old Farm. I hugged them all one by one.

And then I saw her. Cousin Vernon was holding her hand: a small old lady, sprightly and grinning a gummy grin.

"Great-Aunt Vi, you came!" I called.

Great Aunt-Vi laughed giddily. "Yes, my old legs walked off that mountain top and I didn't disappear in a cloud of smoke after all. I never thought I'd see the day when I travelled out of Crooked Bend again. But I decided I couldn't miss another family wedding. I couldn't get to England all those years ago, but I could reach here. And if my brother Bobby can't be here, I told myself, then I should be. Even though I know he will be with us in spirit. I hope you don't mind but I borrowed the stone from the mango tree and brought it here in my pocket, just so it could keep me company on my adventure. But I'll put it back, I promise. Cross my heart..." Then Great Aunt Vi crossed her heart, tapped her pocket and smiled.

I gulped. There was nothing more I could say, except for, "Thank you, Great-Aunt Vi, that means a lot."

I introduced Charley to my cousins, and they all shook her hands and said hello before Dad and Grampie took them all off to freshen up and prepare for the wedding.

Speaking of which, we all had a wedding to get dressed for. And then I realized, *I* had nothing to wear.

Great-Aunt Joy hooked the garment bag over the wardrobe. It was time for the BIG REVEAL of the wedding dress.

This was a huge moment. We'd been through so much with this dress; it was almost beginning to feel like its own person. I felt like giving the thing a name — Claudia? Penelope? No, it felt right to call the dress…Crystal.

Perhaps Crystal the dress would be sparkly — decked out in all the trimmings, like a Christmas tree, with lights hanging from the bodice. I giggled inwardly at the thought. But then I realized something that made me instantly stop. No one had mentioned to Great-Aunt Joy what kind of dress to sew for Mum; we'd left her completely to her own devices. Suppose her tastes were as wild and as dramatic as Auntie Sharon's?

Even though Mum was turning into a chillaxed person, there was still the underlying potential for her to turn into the mother of all bridezillas. What if she hated the dress?

I held my breath.

You could have heard a pin drop in that room. There was silence...

...then gasps.

Mum brought her hands together and pulled them up to her chin in a prayer-like motion as the dress was revealed.

"Well? Cheryl, what do you think?" demanded Glammy Pepper.

Jamaica really was having a funny effect on Mum because she started crying — again.

Did she hate the dress or not? I couldn't tell. She wasn't speaking. She was just staring, her eyes transfixed on Crystal the dress.

Then, through her tears, Mum spoke in hushed tones. "It's absolutely exquisite," she whispered. "Truly, uniquely beautiful, Aunt Joy. I love it. Thank you so, so much."

At this point, I hadn't even looked at the dress. My eyes had been popping out of my head waiting for Mum's reaction. I turned to see it and almost screamed at the sight. In a TOTALLY GOOD WAY. The dress was dream-like. Soft, floaty chiffon flowed effortlessly. An off-the-

shoulder bodice was decorated around the waist with white embroidered roses, with a hint of pale gold around the top of the petals. It was perfection: simple elegance with a touch of glamour, just the way Mum would want it.

Mum went into an adjoining room with Great-Aunt Joy to try the dress on and we waited, fingers crossed hoping that it would fit.

As soon as she saw Mum appear from the room, Auntie Sharon burst into floods of tears. "Oh, stop it, Sharon," commanded Glammy Pepper — and then she got a handkerchief from her handbag and started sobbing too.

There must have been something in the water at breakfast because everyone seemed to be crying.

"Lena? Sunshine? What do you both think?" Mum said turning to us.

"Oh, Mummy, you look like a princess," said Lena gleefully.

"It's a **KNOCKOUT**, Mum," I said. "One hundred per cent — the best dress I've ever seen. And in the past few days, trust me, I've seen a lot of dresses."

Great-Aunt Joy was a genius. She really did know Mum's dress size from a hundred paces. This dress fitted as perfectly as a glove.

Great-Aunt Joy had another surprise in store. Two other concealed packages appeared from out of thin air. How had I not noticed them? She was a magician as well as a genius.

"One for you Lena and one for you Sunshine," she said with a grin wider than the Caribbean Sea.

We hurriedly pulled off the covers as if we were opening birthday presents.

"How did you manage to make these as well?" I asked, deeply in shock.

Two dresses lay on the bed. One a golden puffball, perfect for Lena and her "I'm a happy princess" tastes, and one for me — a shift dress, white and straight, no fuss, with small white roses around the waist, edged with a hint of gold.

"And how did you know what we'd like?" I gasped. "Also, how did you know I had nothing to wear?"

"Heh-hey! I can tell someone's fashion sense in an instant. I also could see that someone was so busy making wedding plans that they would most likely forget they needed something to wear to a secret wedding."

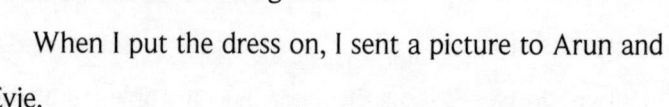

"I knew you could do it, sis! PIECE OF WEDDING CAKE!" shouted Glammy Pepper, which made her and Great-Aunt Joy break out into their Twinzielicious fits of laughter.

When I put the dress on, I sent a picture to Arun and Evie.

A message came back in a zap from Arun. "10 OUT OF 10."

"Sunshine, you look so beautiful," said Mum, which made me feel more than a bit embarrassed.

"Aww, look at our sunny Sunshine. She's getting so grown. If it wasn't for my right-hand woman, none of this would have happened." Auntie Sharon released a long, gooey sniff. "Sunshine's helped organize the cake, the dress, the guest list, and helped me and Tone keep all of this a secret. The girl's been a wonder. You'll make a great leader, just like Nanny of the Maroons. She's a Jamaican national hero, you know."

Mum looked at me in a way I couldn't quite work out. Somewhere between not understanding what was going on and absolute shock. "You've managed to do all this right under my nose without me noticing a thing? Well, apart from you acting a little strangely. But I thought that was a pre-teen thing going on... I'm so proud of you."

If only Mum knew about the near disasters we'd had along the way. Her getting thrown into a swimming pool (well she'd experienced that one herself, but she didn't know it was for the cause); the cake being eaten by Brian and the dogs; failing to find a dress at the shops; almost ordering a school lunch for her wedding meal. I mean, must I go on?

"There were a few hiccups along the way," I told her with a gulp. "Worse than when I tried to pack my suitcase on my own without your help."

"Well, the hiccups make the victories all the sweeter. And you didn't need my help for any of this, did you? I thought I was the chief head of organization, but it looks like we have a new champion in town!" Mum grinned.

"Let's hope I can organize my school stuff as well as this in a few weeks' time, then."

"Sunny, sometimes I nag a lot, I know, that's just what I do. But if this holiday has taught me anything, it is to be more like you," admitted Mum.

"Me?" Mum had been out in the sun far too much on this holiday. Clearly.

She laughed. "Yes, YOU! Never have I met someone so gutsy, so caring and with such a sense of fun. Yes, sometimes things might go wrong. But you have enough spirit and heart to overcome any battle you might face."

"Even my new school?"

Mum looked surprised for a moment but then something clicked into place. "I don't doubt your abilities to achieve anything you set your mind to — and I'm sure you'll be great at your new school. Tell me, what advice would you give me if I were in your shoes?"

I thought about it for a moment. What would Grandad Bobby have said to me? "Don't see it as a battle, see it as an opportunity. An adventure," I told her.

"And I couldn't give better advice myself," said Mum with a watery smile. "Life is always teaching us something new, no matter how old we get. I was hesitant to come back to Jamaica, but now being here, I wished I'd come back sooner."

Mum shook her head slowly.

"I really tried to settle here, you know I did, Mum," she said, looking at Glammy Pepper. "I so wanted it to feel like home, but it was so, so different from Birmingham. It was too hard, and I knew how disappointed you were. But I just couldn't do it. At that age, so young, the change was too much. Somehow Jamaica has managed to stay the same but change a lot too — and so have I. I'm not afraid of change any more." Glammy Pepper wiped at her eyes and nodded, gently. "I know you're facing big changes too,

Sunshine," Mum continued. "And if you need any help, we are here to help you. Always. Just give it your best shot."

"Thanks, Mum. I understand — and I will come to you whenever I need to. I promise. But for now, we should probably make the most of the opportunity right in front of us and get you married to Dad. Again."

28

THE CEREMONY

Miss Babette tapped a sparkling orange fingernail onto her golden watch.

"Two o'clock on the dot. SHOW TIME!" she sang.

Miss Babette was dressed to impress in a crisp, navy trouser suit and frilly pale-orange shirt. Despite the heat, she seemed as cool as a cucumber, the panic of the last few days erased from her memory.

"This is *your* day. Enjoy it," Miss Babette said to Mum, with a gleaming smile. "Your family have gone to so much effort, especially this one." Miss Babette nodded in my direction. "She's destined to be a prime minister one day, I tell you. That's if she doesn't make her citizens eat chips with every meal." She winked at me.

Chips with every meal? I couldn't think of anything better.

"To your stations, please, ladies." Miss Babette snapped back into work mode.

Lena was first in line with her golden puffball dress, holding Betty the Bat in one hand and Brown Bunny in the other. I followed behind her in my white shift dress, and Auntie Sharon, who was behind me as chief bridesmaid, wore a glittering golden, strappy, straight dress. We all carried little bouquets of white and orange flowers.

Glammy Pepper wore an embroidered black and gold jacket, golden blouse and flared black trousers — and Mum, in her elegant wedding gown, had a garland of orange and white flowers in her hair.

"Let's do this for Daddy, hey, Chez," said Auntie Sharon.

Mum nodded and smiled.

Glammy Pepper stepped forward and slipped one arm through Mum's arm. Mum had asked Glammy to escort her down the aisle. This was a HUGE move by Mum as she and Glammy Pepper have always had what a grown-up might call a "difficult relationship". Glammy looked as if she could burst with pride.

Lilting music began to play from somewhere nearby and we stepped out from the back of the hotel lobby into glorious sunshine onto a walkway sprinkled with flower petals, the golden beach either side of us. We walked past our family and friends: Mrs Turner, Godmother Patsy, Great-Aunt Joy, Ziggy, Lorna, Miss Winnie, Chef B (resisting the temptation to burst into song), Granny Cynthie, Grampie Clive, Daz and Tiffany from Texas, my cousins from Crooked Bend, including Great-Aunt Vi, and Charley with her bob of bright red hair. Dad's side of the family had also arrived from another part of the island too, and Auntie Sharon was paying for them to stay the rest of the week with us – and then, ANOTHER SURPRISE. I almost fell off the walkway in shock.

I recognized the familiar curls, not pushed up and out of the way in a ponytail, but flying free. The curly head turned in my direction and a brilliant smile flashed at me as glorious as the afternoon sun.

EVIE. Evie was at the secret wedding! Next to Evie sat her mum and dad, who were beaming at us too.

Charley and Evie giggled as they saw my face. My mouth was so wide open I could have caught a swarm of flies (or mosquitoes). My brain couldn't quite compute how this was all happening. I wanted to stop right there and then in the middle of our bridal walk to ask **HOW IN THE WORLD** did Evie get here? But I had to focus. (Also, I didn't want to ruin the wedding by causing Auntie Sharon, Mum and Glammy Pepper to tumble down like dominoes if I made a sudden emergency stop.)

I continued smiling and walking, and that's when I noticed Dad. He was standing ahead of us, underneath a white canopy, draped with white curtains and bunches of flowers tied around them. Peter stood next to him. Both were dressed in smart blue suits. Because we'd forgotten about their wedding day clothes too, the hotel had helped us out by arranging rented suits. Dad beamed that goofy smile of his as he saw us approaching. I smiled my widest smile back at him.

I love my dad. He's easy-going and kind, and as much

as this secret wedding had been for Mum, all the effort was worth it for him as well. My parents can go on and on about loads of random stuff, nagging, telling us what to do, et cetera, et cetera — which is obviously a bit annoying at times — but I wouldn't literally be me without them and I was glad that they both looked so happy and young again, right here in this moment.

When Mum and Dad were together underneath the canopy, they held hands (a little yuck, but okay) and said their vows, sharing soppy nice words about each other. Dad had found something original to say without quoting

Shakespeare or other long-gone old poets. Mum, being Mum, managed to write her words and recite them perfectly within the twenty-four hours of knowing she'd be getting married again.

So, finally, Mum and Dad renewed their vows. We'd got to this point after only two-and-a-bit weeks of planning.

PHEW! Our work was done.

The "Grand Hall" where we held the wedding reception looked spectacular. Grampie and Daz, with the help of Miss Babette's wedding team, had dressed it to impress. I don't mean to throw shade here, but Daz was a better wedding dresser than wedding-dress shopper.

"Y'all so funny," said Tiffany when I'd mentioned that. Daz just looked at me like he wanted to push me into one of the swimming pools.

Orange paper lanterns floated delicately from the ceiling, dotted between two elegant chandeliers. The Twinzies had made paper chains of orange snowflakes (because only the Twinzies would adorn a summer wedding with a winter theme), but they added that offbeat touch that perfectly sums up the energy of my family with all our little quirky bits that make us, us.

The guest tables were
all dressed to match, with
crisp white tablecloths, and glass
vases filled with orange, yellow
and white flowers as centrepieces.
Little bags filled with gold and orange
sweets and mints, called favours, were at each place
setting, with glinting crystal glasses, concertinaed gold
napkins, and polished golden cutlery completing the look.
The chairs were dressed in white covers with golden bows
tied around them. Auntie Sharon commented that the
room would have been even better with a dash of leopard
print. "But you can't have it all!" she said, with a shrug.
Mum and Dad smiled at each other, probably in relief that
that there was no animal print in sight.

I finally had time to go over to Evie before we sat down
to eat. "I don't mean to be funny or anything, but WHAT
ARE YOU DOING HERE?"

Her face fell but then I grinned and hugged her.

"We were in the Caribbean, anyway," started Evie,
excitedly, "but then the ship stopped off in Jamaica, so

we're here for the day, but leave tomorrow. It's like PERFECT TIMING."

Only Evie could have a tale to tell like that.

"You did an excellent job organizing all this, Sunny. Everything looks brilliant, I knew you could do it."

"You did?" I said in surprise.

"Yes of course! I don't know why you doubt yourself so much, Sunshine Simpson."

Well, that was true. Guilty as charged.

"You know, when I first found out I wasn't going to Beeches Grammar, I thought it was a joke — that my parents were playing a very unfunny trick on me," Evie confessed. "But then when I realized they weren't joking, it felt deadly serious. Even though I really like Greenhill Academy, I'd worked so hard preparing myself for grammar school tests for so many years. I've always been so sure I wouldn't fail at anything."

"But you didn't fail, Evie," I protested. "You're one of the smartest people I've ever met."

"Yes, that's true," said Evie confidently. I smiled, glad that the Evie I knew so well was still very much alive and kicking. "I didn't fail. I tried my absolute best, trying to be the best. And I don't think there's anything wrong in that. If anything, I think I overworked myself, put myself under too much pressure. Trying to be the perfect student. Trying to make my parents proud."

"Your parents are super proud of you, Evie. I see that any time I spend time with you. You're—"

"So, what I'm trying to say, Sunshine," said Evie, cutting me off mid-sentence. "I think you put yourself under too much pressure, just like me. And you doubt yourself too much – which, I must admit, isn't like me. Go to Beeches Grammar and do great. You'll make new friends who will like you as much as Arun, Charley and I do.

"You've helped me to see the lighter side of things and to give myself a break, but you don't always do that for yourself. I'm going to Greenhill Academy to be great, and you'll be great too. Stop second-guessing yourself and just be you."

She smiled. I knew Evie had ended her pep talk on a bossy note on purpose, because that's Evie. But everything she said was true. I couldn't deny it. I nodded.

We'd both come a long way in our friendship. I had much to learn from Evie too, especially her confidence and self-assuredness.

"I guess I've been worried that it will be disappointing. Just all too new, especially without my friends there. I've had a few wobbles over the past few weeks," I admitted.

"Well. You never know until you try. And for goodness' sake, HAVE FUN and make new friends — but don't forget your old friends!"

"You're right, Evie. As always."

"I know," said Evie with a wry smile.

We couldn't help but laugh.

After our wedding meal of delicious Caribbean food and chips, it was time to cut the wedding cake. It had thick white icing with white and golden roses made out of fondant around the sides — and a little silver horseshoe on top for luck. Chef B had done a fantastic job.

"I could see this cake gracing the best restaurants in Paris. You have so much international flair," I told him.

Chef B's eyes lit up. He opened his mouth as if he was about to burst into song, but I put my fingers to my lips and smiled. It was time for Dad to make a speech.

"Cheryl, you look absolutely stunning. How lucky I am to get to celebrate being married to you for fifteen years. And here we are, at last, in Jamaica, with our family and friends around us. We know there is someone incredibly special who isn't with us today. Cheryl's dad, Bobby, was at our first wedding and walked her down the aisle. But we are truly blessed that there are other special people in our lives, not present on our original wedding day, who are here now — and, luckily for us, we have children who carry their grandfather with them. In Peter's cheekiness and sweetness, in Lena's kindness of heart — and in Sunshine... well, Sunshine is the complete embodiment of her grandfather and we're so proud of her. She holds her head up high, even when she doesn't always feel that she can. Because that's the beautiful thing about this family. We don't always win, but we never quit."

"Except when we win the lottery!" cried Auntie Sharon.

Everyone cracked up laughing. "We've got you," continued Dad, looking at Mum. "We've got each other." Dad paused for another moment, before finishing his speech. "And if Grandad Bobby were here now, he would *say 'stop talking, yuh chat too much, have a glass of rum for me'*."

We all laughed again; Grandad would definitely have said something like that. Dad held up his glass and then everyone else held their glasses up too, in a toast.

"To treasured memories and to new beginnings," said Dad.

"To treasured memories and to new beginnings," we all chorused.

Dad was right. I could see parts of Grandad Bobby in my siblings, in Mum and Auntie Sharon — and in me. I didn't need the Jamaica stone to remember Grandad. He was everywhere, and I would do my very best to never let the joy he carried in his spirit fade away.

Once the speeches were done, the wedding DJ hit the decks. It was the same DJ who was at the pool the day Mum fell in. When Auntie Sharon had asked him to DJ at the wedding reception, he'd said *"it would be an honour to play music at the wedding of the greatest pool party queen I've ever seen"*, which pleased Mum no end when we'd told her.

"And now it's time for the happy couple's first dance," he said. "And we have someone very special to announce it." The DJ stepped out of the way, and a projector screen came down from the ceiling. A video started to play, and there was a chorus of gasps in the room as a tall, familiar man appeared and said a few words.

"Congratulations to Tony and Cheryl on your special day. This song is for you..." said none other than Mum's favourite film star, Idris Elba, with a brilliant smile. Auntie Sharon had asked if he could record a special video message for Mum on the day we'd met him in the hotel lobby.

Mum and Godmother Patsy screamed and started flapping their arms about uncontrollably. Honestly, grown-ups can be so embarrassing sometimes.

"Um, should we have our first dance?" Dad asked Mum, not sure whether she was going to run screaming towards the big screen and try to dive into it.

"Tony, there's no one I'd rather dance with than you," said Mum, calming herself down, which was all a bit soppy and EMOSH.

But, anyway, after the first dance, it was time to PAARTAAY!!!!

Ziggy, Chef B and Peter were challenging each other to see who had the best dance moves. They whipped themselves into a frenzy to a song called "Toast". Dennis joined in too. He may be quieter than Auntie Sharon, but he came alive at the wedding. He was dressed to impress, in trousers with seams so sharp you could cut your fingers on them, an embroidered blue and gold waistcoat and shiny blue and white striped shoes. He was literally dazzling on the dance floor — and then Auntie Sharon joined him, calling me over.

"Come on, Sunshine, let's show 'em how it's done!" she exclaimed.

I stood next to her and Dennis, and then the DJ started playing a song called "Candy" by this ancient group called Cameo. All the wedding guests, including my grandparents and even Great-Aunt Vi, flooded the dance floor and followed the moves that Auntie Sharon and I were doing. We call it the Candy dance, but the moves were originally done to a song called "Electric Boogie" also known as the "Electric Slide", Dad told us afterwards. (There's always a history lesson with my dad — even at a wedding!)

In the dance, we took two steps to the right and two steps to the left, and then two steps back, before leaning backwards onto one foot, then forwards onto the other foot, leaning backwards again, and then hopping and jumping to the right, and repeating the actions again and again until the song was over.

It's hard to describe on paper, but you've just got to try the Candy dance!

Auntie Sharon got into the swing of things then, the trouble with her mosquito-bitten leg forgotten. She led us in a conga line to an old SOCA song called "Hot Hot Hot". The whole wedding party went on a lap around the dance floor, out of the room, around the lobby and then back into the reception, picking up other people, who were innocently minding their own business, along the way.

I got so HOT HOT HOT from all the dancing that I stepped back out into the lobby, with Charley and Evie, just to catch my breath and give Arun a quick video call. His mum and dad had let him stay up late so I could update him on the wedding.

"AWESOME wedding," said Arun. "And you'll definitely need to teach me the moves to the Candy dance when we're back home."

Trust Arun to have dance moves at the forefront of his mind.

A man with silver hair passed by with some other people.

Evie and Charley started pointing, grinning wildly and waving.

The man with silver hair nodded, waved and smiled.

"Do you know who that was?" asked Evie, with widened eyes.

"No. Who?"

"THAT was George Clooney!" she announced.

I didn't recognize the name at first and then I twigged. "Oh, that's George Gooney. The actor you saw in Italy when you were on holiday? He gets everywhere, doesn't he?!"

"Actually, his name is George…Ooh, never mind. You are amazing Sunshine Simpson; do you know that?" Evie grinned.

"Sunshine is the best!" agreed Charley.

"One in a million!" called Arun down the phone.

"And you, Charley, Arun and Evie are the greatest friends of all! **ALWAYS** and **FOR EVER!**" I chimed.

"May the wind always be at our backs and the sun shine warm on our faces," said Charley.

Evie, Arun and I shared confused looks.

"It's an old Irish blessing wishing us all well," Charley confirmed.

"I love it, Charley. Thank you."

299

Charley stood in the middle, and Evie and I were either side of her as we walked onto the beach, linking arms. I held my phone up with my free arm so that Arun  could see what was going on. After another ten minutes or so of chatting about our holidays, Arun let out a long, dramatic yawn. To be fair, it was late — the early morning hours for him! We waved him goodbye and then Evie and Charley went to explore the beach further, while I stayed behind. I needed time and a bit of space to take in the day's events. This whole holiday had been so much fun but kind of exhausting and overwhelming at the same time.

In fact, so much had happened in the past year. I'd left primary school, I was about to move on to high school, my aunt had become a millionaire — and my grandad had died.

But this holiday — and the wedding — had helped me to realize something about my grief. It's not that I missed my grandad any less, it's just that life had grown around my sadness and cushioned the blow a little.

At times, I'd feel scared and lonely and worried and angry, and at other times I'd cry, with tears of joy as well as sadness — because life is a mixed bag like that. And now, here I was in Jamaica finding happiness in new experiences and overcoming challenges in my own haphazard way, but I'd got through it. Because every day is a new day — and it's what we make of it that counts.

It wasn't just the fancy hotel and all its trimmings that had made this holiday special. It was my friends — old and new — and my family who had been the cherry on top of Chef B's and Granny Cynthie's perfectly-iced wedding cake.

Later on, when night fell, I watched the twinkling stars as they lit up the sky. My Grandad Bobby once told me that whenever he got lonely, he would look up at the stars and know he was never far away from home. Seeing the stars now, I knew exactly what he meant. I was almost five thousand miles away from England, but home was still all around — and there were new adventures waiting for me when I did travel back across the night-stained inky ocean.

Maybe when I started at my new school, I would be able to adapt to new situations. Maybe it would be hard, maybe it would be easy, or maybe somewhere in between the two. There was only one way to find out. And, as I'd learned along the way, with help from my family and friends, I shouldn't overthink things too much — I should just be.

Bob Marley's famous song "Three Little Birds" filled my mind. Now wasn't the time to focus on tomorrow. It was time to live for today and to enjoy the treasures that were right in front of me — and I had every intention of making the most of the rest of my time left here in this joyful paradise.

The trip to Jamaica was my greatest adventure so far, but there would be more to come. Right now, I felt happy and content in my grandparents' home. My second home. A wondrous home.

THE END

Sunshine's Jamaican Fact File

DID YOU KNOW?

Jamaica has three main counties: Cornwall, Middlesex and Surrey. Do these names sound familiar? There are fourteen parishes across the three counties, including Clarendon, which Sunshine travels to on her holiday. Other places in the story including Marine Bay, Crystal Cove Falls and Crooked Bend in the River are fictional, but are inspired by some beautiful parts of the island.

DID YOU KNOW?

Jamaica has close links with Britain (you can probably tell by the names of the Jamaican counties). Jamaica became an independent country on the 6th of August 1962. The day is known as Jamaican Independence Day and is a national holiday in Jamaica.

DID YOU KNOW?

Jamaica's national flag stands out from the crowd. The colours of the flag are black, gold and green. Most other countries in the world feature red, white or blue.

DID YOU KNOW?

When it rains in Jamaica it can really pour! In 1988, Hurricane Gilbert was one of the most devastating storms to ever hit the island. It caused major damage to the country and many people were hurt or killed.

DID YOU KNOW?

Jamaica has seven national heroes, including Nanny of the Maroons (Queen Nanny). Who are your heroes?

DID YOU KNOW?

James Bond is Jamaican – sort of (ish)! The writer of the James Bond books, Ian Fleming, fell in love with the country and wrote his James Bond books at his home on the island.

Sunshine's Holiday Dos and Don'ts

✳ **DON'T** throw your grown—up – or anyone else – into a swimming pool. This could be dangerous.

✳ **DO** keep your delicious snacks away from greedy goats.

✳ **DON'T** leave anyone home alone.

✳ **DO** have fun!

✳ **DON'T** forget your toothbrush!

G.M. LINTON lives with her family in the West Midlands and can often be found happily snacking on stuffed green olives or hunting out a slice of cake. She enjoys nothing better than snatching time to read a good book and losing herself whilst imagining characters and storylines.

The **SUNSHINE SIMPSON** series is particularly inspired by G.M.'s parents, who arrived in Britain, from Jamaica, as part of the Windrushgeneration, in the 1950s.

ACKNOWLEDGEMENTS

I can't believe I'm here writing the acknowledgements for Sunshine Simpson's third adventure. It's been quite a journey since 2017, when I began writing the first book, and I have many people to thank for helping me along the way.

My superstar agent, Claire Wilson, has never stopped championing Sunshine — and me. And Safae El-Ouahabi spins many plates so gracefully. Thank you for your support.

The whole team at Usborne, including my brilliant editors Rebecca Hill, Anne Finnis, and Stephanie King (who copy-edited the book), are insightful and wise, and make sense of my nonsense. Fritha Lindqvist and Beth Gardner work wonders with publicity and marketing — and help me to look like I know what I'm doing, which is quite the task. They truly are miracle workers.

Huge thanks to Fuuji Takashi who has brought Sunshine to life on the page through her gorgeous illustrations. I loved her artwork from the moment I first saw it. What an extraordinary talent she is. Thanks also to Asma Enayeh for the exceptional additional illustrations, which add such warmth and extra interest. Designers Will Steele and Sarah Cronin have also worked so hard to bring the cover and insides together. They have done a brilliant job — the design is truly glorious. And thanks to Gareth Collinson and Charlotte James for their expert proofreading, and to Beth Wetherfield for her insightful comments on an earlier version of this book.

One of the hardest parts of writing a story is letting go and watching it fly out into the world to do its thing and find its readership. I have been fortunate enough in the past year to have been longlisted and shortlisted for awards, including the Waterstones Children's Book Prize, and to have received national and local press coverage. I appreciate it all, greatly.

Thank you to everyone who has embraced Sunshine, and her family and friends, and especially those who have stuck with her through thick and thin during all her adventures.

To the booksellers, bloggers, librarians, journalists, teachers and reviewers who have read the book(s), thank you! I see you and appreciate what you do, not just for my book, but for the time and effort you put into reading and promoting all kinds of children's literature, year in year out. But then who wouldn't want to? Children's literature is THE BEST — you are not only brilliant but incredibly wise.

I was semi-reluctant to name names here, because so many people have been so kind, but I do want to give a special mention to Chris Soul, Jacqui Sydney and Joanne Owen. Thank you for your support.

I had every intention of writing a story where Sunshine would visit Jamaica, as part of the series. Jamaica is the home of my parents and ancestors, and I am so proud to include this "likkle but tallawah" island in the story. Though I may have taken artistic licence with the names of some locations and descriptions, hopefully the story gives a flavour of the natural beauty of the island.

My parents came to England in the 1950s, leaving their immediate families behind. They never did return to live "back home" but built up a network of extended family and friends in Britain, who would provide support for each other over many decades. Thank you to the Alexander family, Bonnick family, Chambers family, Clarke family, Dwyer family, Ebanks family, Hemmings family, Howe family, Landell family, Linton family, Matthews family, Palmer family, Porter family, Reid family, Smikle family, Stewart family, Wright family — and more. That's a lot of families! But, truly, my childhood would not have been the same without them. Even now, they still show such care, loyalty and support.

And to all my aunts, uncles and cousins in Jamaica, America, Canada, and throughout the Caribbean, we may be oceans apart, but you will always mean so much.

A special thank you to all the authors who took time

out of their own busy writing schedules — and lives — to provide quotes of support. Aisha Bushby, Jen Carney, A.M. Dassu, Hannah Gold, L.D. Lapinski, Ṭọlá Okogwu, Serena Patel, Rashmi Sirdeshpande and Lisa Thompson, I can't convey how deeply your kind words have furrowed into my being and stayed with me.

To Sue — thanks for buying copies for your family members and getting them to say lovely things about the series (I hope you didn't pay them!). And thanks to all my friends and colleagues who have bought copies and spread the word about Sunshine everywhere.

Special thanks to Candi, Luke, Thai and Aria who gave me live commentary from Jamaica while I was drafting the book. One love!

Thanks to Rose, Ivor, Hilary, Alison, Mimi, Lissy, Mikey and Russell — and all my nieces and nephews. They tell me the whole truth (and nothing but the truth) but also pick me up and dust me down when I fall. Alison has very kindly read every draft of the series and has been meticulous and spot on in her feedback. And Hilary is my sales champion extraordinaire!

I give thanks to God, who none of this would be possible without. And one more mention of my dear parents. A thousand books wouldn't be enough to thank them for all they did for me. This is for them — and, by extension, the Windrush generation.

Lastly, thank you to all Sunshine Simpson readers — young or old(er). Whether this is the first, second or third book in the series you have read, it means the world. It always will.

LOOK OUT FOR SUNSHINE'S EARLIER ADVENTURES:

Sunshine Simpson's larger-than-life Grandad is always telling her to get out and find her own adventures, but unfortunately BAD LUCK has a habit of coming her way.

Her new friend Evie is fast becoming a FRENEMY, her home haircut is a DISASTER, and the school showcase is so STRESSFUL! Everything seems to be going wrong! Especially with Grandad getting older every week.

Sunshine needs to find her voice, but can she break through the clouds to stand tall, stand proud, and show the world she can shine?

EVERY CLOUD HAS A SILVER LINING

USBORNE

SUNSHINE SIMPSON
COOKS UP A STORM

"Officially a new favourite."
TOLÁ OKOGWU

Fun factfiles and recipe inside!

G.M. LINTON

Sunshine Simpson's life has never been so busy! She feels like she's on a ROLLERCOASTER.

At school everyone is talking about preparing for the big move to SCARY secondary. Plus, there's a Charity Bake Sale to plan for.

But with Sunshine's Dad travelling for work, Mum forgetting how to smile, a surprise family guest in the mix, and her BFFs and bake-sale classmate Riley CLASHING, Sunshine needs a DARING PLAN to stop the storm clouds from settling!

Will Sunshine's foolproof plan prove to be a piece of CAKE...or a recipe for disaster?

EVERYONE LOVES SUNSHINE